I0748422

HOME MOVIES

by

Joel Momberg

Published by Born Young Publishers
P.O. Box 7161
St. Petersburg, FL 33734
www.iwasbornveryyoung.com

ISBN 978-0-578-51464-2

To the hundreds of students that I had the honor of teaching. As their teacher, I realize now how much more they taught me.

"Power does not corrupt men;
fools, however, if they get into a position of power,
corrupt power."

—*George Bernard Shaw*

FOREWORD

When I was 25 years old, I lived for a brief time in Vienna, Austria and taught at the American International School. It was an interesting place. Students from the United States and from just about every country in the world attended. Many of these kids were from diplomatic families and (thankfully) all spoke English. I was there on a temporary assignment to teach college prep and study skills.

It was there that I met and befriended a terrific teacher, Karl Tremmel. Karl taught kindergarten, which was unusual for a man. He had a big personality and was a favorite with both teachers and students. Although his methods were unorthodox, his results were stellar.

Karl became the inspiration for Karl "Buddy" Rosen, the main character of my novel Home Movies.

Much of Karl's teaching style and personality is captured in this book. He did, in fact, have a classroom with built-in ledges, where students nestled to read and a library filled with books for young and old. And every Saturday, Karl would visit the big flea market in the middle of town to buy "treasures" like old train watches and books and—yes—home movies. He would run these movies for his students in class and they would make up stories of what they saw: birthday parties, amusement rides and summer vacations.

I had many fond memories of Karl.

When my time at AIS was coming to a close and I really wanted to stay longer, the headmaster asked all the teachers if anyone would be interested in teaching seventh-grade history for the remainder of the year.

"Momberg will do it!" Karl offered. I was stunned. I had no idea how to teach history to seventh graders. Sadly, the teacher who had been teaching the course had been the victim of a fatal car crash on the Autobahn. A substitute had been watching the class for the last few weeks.

I sat in silence as the headmaster looked in my direction. "That right? You want to give it a try?"

"Well ... um ... can you tell me what are they studying this semester?" I asked, as if that would make a difference in my decision.

"Japanese history." He answered. Oh great, I thought. Japanese history! There was no way ...

"C'mon man. I know you can do that. I'll even help you get through it." I heard Karl say behind me patting me on the shoulder. "He's in."

"Okay then. That's settled. Thank you Mr. Momberg." The headmaster smiled. "And of course Mr. Tremmel ... your agent!"

That semester was one of the more interesting ones in my life. Karl and I visited the Japanese Embassy and picked up pamphlets and books on Japanese government, Japanese papermaking, Japanese gardens. You name it, we found something on it.

I assigned every student a topic and they, in turn, presented it to the class each week. We all took notes and I learned more than they did that year.

Karl and I remained friends when I returned home to Florida. He taught school with me for the next few years in a private elementary school in St. Petersburg. The students all adored him and his quirky ways served him well.

The journey that Buddy Rosen takes in Home Movies is not one that Karl took in real life. I'd like to think, however, that his spirit of adventure lives on in Buddy Rosen and brings this story to life.

Enjoy!

CONTENTS

FADE-IN:

Private Hell of Bernie Abraham

The pillows didn't help.

His back still ached and he had the taste of bile still in his mouth from vomiting over an hour ago. There was nothing in his stomach except the last few slugs of Seagrams and a stale pretzel or two. The doctor told him to take the thiamin that sat unopened on the coffee table. "What's the difference?" he thought, "I'll just throw it up with the other stuff."

Bernie Abraham's house was as rundown as he was. The light bothered his eyes, so he kept the windows closed up with heavy curtains that kept out any hint of the sun. The taxicab he owned didn't move during the day anymore. He picked up fares only at night. Lately, food didn't interest him; so shopping was necessary only when he ran out of alcohol, which happened more frequently. Nighttime visits to the liquor store were regular stops after he dropped his last passenger.

He sat in his easy chair staring at the mute television set flickering in the corner. He no longer cared what was on. He just looked at the pictures on the screen. On top of the television was the only picture he displayed. It was a family shot of him, his wife and his son.

He reached over and snapped on the switch to an old movie projector that sat on the coffee table at his feet. The light flashed and the wall came alive.

... a blurred closeup of a gap-toothed grin gleams full frame. The camera pulls back to catch the full face and the full body. The boy is dressed in a baseball shirt opened and untucked with a red tee shirt underneath. Embroidered across the chest is "Indians." His red cap has the handmade trifold brim cocked low over his eyes. It barely covers the thick, blond hair that sticks out the front and sides. Rolled-up blue jeans and black high top sneakers show the dirt stains from a recent slide. He's swinging his bat for the camera. He does this about six times and then poses in a Willie Mays stance...

A smile broke out on Bernie's face. He sat up straighter and adjusted his pillows.

... a ball comes into camera view suddenly from the right and hits the boy in the shoulder. He looks around and angrily throws down his bat. He runs in the direction of the throw. The camera follows as he jumps on the laughing player who threw the ball. The boy is surprised as he is punched in the stomach and in the chest. The other boy takes a swing. They wrestle on the ground...

Bernie laughed, "Temper, temper, Buddy Boy. You're just like your old man."

... the cameraman says something to the boys. They look up, still holding on to each other's jersey. After a few seconds, they brush themselves off and reluctantly shake hands. They

both smile and punch each other in the arms. Then the first boy picks up his bat and heads to the dugout...

Bernie turned off the projector. He sat for a minute in darkness then restarted it.

... the dad moves into the picture. He and the boy look so much alike. He's dressed in a baseball cap with "Coach" embroidered on it. He slaps the boy down to the ground and wags a finger at him. He then kicks him hard in the stomach as the boy grimaces in pain...

"Play ball!" Bernie said as a mock toast, the bottle of Seagrams in his hand. A small tear dripped down his right cheek.

... the cameraman hands the camera to a kid in the infield and runs over to help out. Most of the action is still in the frame but not quite centered and a little unsteady in the new hands. The cameraman turns out to really be a camerawoman. It's the boy's mother. She rushes to help the boy and holds back the flailing father. She gets knocked down and holds on to the man's leg. He continues to yell at the boy and tries to shake off the woman. He suddenly stops as if a ball hit him in the head and looks around. He picks the woman up off the ground; the boy brushes himself off again as mother recaptures the camera. Dad drops a bottle out of his back pocket. He picks it up and almost trips over his own feet... the film breaks...

"Abe, you always were an asshole." He raised the empty bottle to his lips.

Bernie threw it at the wall and smashed it to pieces.

CUT TO:

Buddy's Big Discovery Leads to Big Trouble

Six-year-old Joshua Ferguson stood facing the center of the courtyard at morning assembly as he came to the end of The Pledge of Allegiance … kinda.

"… and one nation divisible … AMEN."

It was a time-honored tradition at Coquina Preparatory School. The flag that stood on the tarnished stand always looked like it was just about to fall over and topple the podium that school principal Linda Rankin used every morning promptly at 8:04 A.M.

"Thank you, Joshua," Miss Rankin said as she addressed the assembly. "That was simply divine. Now let's recognize our birthday celebrants. Would you all come forward?"

As Linda Rankin's voice prattled on, Karl "Buddy" Rosen, Joshua's teacher, let his mind slowly drift and hover between the cup of coffee he missed that morning and the long, tan legs that belonged to Andi Fenimore, the art teacher across the courtyard from where he stood. It didn't go unnoticed. Andi looked over at Buddy and licked her lips sensually. He felt heat rush to every part of his body.

"Parents' Night will be this Thursday. A notice will be handed out in your classrooms so be sure to bring it home to your parents."

Buddy mouthed the words: I want you in Andi's direction. She wrinkled her eyebrows as if she didn't understand him. Bob Kevin didn't miss it. He looked over at Buddy from the other side of the courtyard and mouthed: I want you, too. Buddy, in turn, mouthed *fuck you* and stuck out his tongue at Kevin.

"Lunch today is macaroni and cheese, hot dog, vegetable medley and vanilla ice cream cup."

Buddy's kindergarten class had an attention span of about two minutes and morning assembly reduced it to less than half that time. They were already finished picking everything off their bodies and had started on their friends' bodies.

Buddy felt a tug on his thumb. "... And he wiped it right on my sleeve, Mr. Rosen," Hillary Greenstein whined.

"What was that, Hillary?" asked Buddy.

"Steven put a big disgusting booger on me."

"What did you do?"

"I flicked it on him!"

"Seems only fair."

"Um, Mr. Rosen," Miss Rankin said into the microphone as it squealed loudly, "is there a problem there?"

"No, Miss Rankin," Buddy said. Then he muttered, "Nothing a little kleenex can't fix."

"Very well," Miss Rankin replied and then turned to the rest of the assembly, "Now, students, don't forget to be prompt and attentive this afternoon when you arrive at the bus lane or the car pool lane and have a glooorious day."

Buddy turned to Hillary and Steven as they started to leave. "Who wants to apologize first?"

They both shook hands and headed back to the classroom. Steven managed to flick another booger as Buddy's back was turned. Hillary punched Steven hard in the back.

"Hey, Rosen," Kevin called to him before Buddy disappeared into his classroom. "You got a booger on your back."

Buddy pretended to wipe it off and flick it at him. "... must be yours."

Buddy looked over his small charges and smiled. He really loved his job. Sure, there were the normal day-to-day stresses that come with teaching and certainly there were the days that he could ring their adorable little necks. But, overall he'd rather do this than anything in the world.

He walked over to Stacey Barnes, "Okay, Stacey, you're on for today as Marion the Math Maiden."

Stacey headed for the Math Castle, a platform Buddy built in one corner of his room supported by four wooden columns four feet tall. Wide stairs covered with indoor/outdoor carpeting led to the top. It was ringed by a plywood castle wall. "What about the Merry Math Men?" Stacey asked as she ascended the stairs.

"Let's take a look at the list." Buddy read from the paper of assignments tacked to the wall behind the climbing pole that doubled as the Sherwood Forest Tree of Knowledge. The tree extended through the center of a hole in the Castle floor.

"Looks like it's Little John Stanley ... Friar Thomas Foley ... and Robin Robert Dowling." Buddy read. "Front and center, Merry Men. Here are your assignments: Today is the day to give to the poor. Divide your treasures. Give 20 gold pieces to each of our 21 townspeople." Stacey and the three Merry Men dove under the platform to search the huge assortment of blocks, dolls, puzzles, marbles and such.

Buddy moved to the special reading corner. It really should have been called a prereading corner, since the students weren't really reading at this age. They were looking at pictures and starting to understand what the words meant. Six students in the morning reading group grabbed their favorite books and squeezed onto two benches from a 1971 VW van that Buddy had owned in Austria. On either side were plastic baskets and apple crates lying on their sides and stacked to hold every kind of book imaginable. Lewis Carroll and Harriet Beecher Stowe were mixed in with Shakespeare, Dickens and even Edgar Allen Poe. Old editions of World Book Encyclopedias, "Where the Wild Things Are" and "Plumbing Made Simple" shared equal billing.

On the opposite wall, three antique coat racks filled with coats, costumes, hats and bags were getting a workout from the remaining ten kindergartners. There were no desks in the classroom. Director's chairs, rockers, lounge chairs and lots of kid sized tables and chairs were scattered around. The center of the room was open and covered by a massive oriental rug.

There was only one rule in Buddy's classroom: TO SHARE. It was posted on all the walls and in 15 different languages. Buddy spent hours on that concept. These were the selfish years, or, as Buddy called it, The Memine Times. He was a firm believer in selflessness. He learned it the hard way. He was determined not to let that happen to his young students.

Miss Rankin, who had walked in unannounced and unnoticed, tapped Buddy on the shoulder. "Mr. Rosen, could you step out in the hallway for a second?"

Buddy swung around, surprised by the visitor. "Sure Miss Rankin." He turned back to his class, "Kids, I'm going to be right outside."

Robert interrupted him, "Can I feed Shithead?"

Miss Rankin's eyes grew to the size of big marbles. Buddy jumped in quickly, "No, Robert , he eats later in the day. And his name is Voltaire, remember?" Buddy saw Rankin's face and explained, "He gets confused. We had a lesson last week about snakes. Voltaire is our resident python. His skin shedded and Robert thinks I called him shithead ."

"I see." Miss Rankin remained skeptical. They stepped outside the door and left it cracked enough to see the children. "Mr. Rosen, you know that the Accreditation Committee will be doing their annual site visits next week. "

"I know," Buddy answered. "We prepared a special program just for their visit. Billy Moore and Fred Washington wrote a one act play called Sounds My Body Makes. Of course, some of it had to be censored."

"Mr. Rosen, that's just what I wanted to talk to you about. Since you've been here, we have had many discussions about your, well, unorthodox methods of teaching. I know you are doing marvelous things with the students and they absolutely adore you. But we are very conservative here. Some of the board members are upset about your methods and with the Accreditation Committee's visit, I just wanted you to be, well, careful."

"Careful?" Buddy asked knowing very well what Miss Rankin meant, but enjoyed watching her squirm a little.

"Yes. I mean with what you say and do and ... what you wear."

"My wardrobe isn't appropriate, either?"

Miss Rankin blushed. "It's nap time I'm talking about."

"I always observe nap time."

"I know you do. You observe it too well. In all the years I've been a teacher and a principal I have never met anyone who takes a nap with his class ... and wears pajamas, to boot."

"Don't forget my Teddy. I always sleep with my Teddy."

"You sleep with a Teddy?"

Hillary the Snitch interrupted. "Mr. Rosen, Steven took off his pants."

"Uh, oh. Last time he did that we had to evacuate the building. Sorry, Miss Rankin, I gotta run."

"Mr. Rosen, I'm not finished."

Buddy shook hands, "I certainly enjoy our special moments together, Miss Rankin, but I have to get my kids to Music Class now. Good day."

"But," as the door closed, Miss Rankin sighed, "Well, I never!"

Buddy put his feet up on the old scratched table that was reflective of the rest of the decor that adorned the Teacher's Lounge. He read a SpiderMan comic book with the catchy title, THE AMAZING SPIDERMAN: THE INVASION OF THE SPIDER SLAYERS PART TWO OF SIX !

"I saw your lips move, Rosen." Bob Kevin knocked Buddy's feet off the table as he put his books down.

"Hey, you're not fooling me with those books. Everybody knows you haven't learned to read yet."

"Have too! Tomorrow I start Cat In the, what's that word, Heat?" Kevin poured the remaining drops of coffee into his mug with the slogan, Those Who Can, Teach. He pulled up a chair next to Buddy.

"Look at this, Kevin," Buddy said to him, "Peter Parker meets his parents in this issue. But he's not sure whether they're really his parents. They were political prisoners for 20 years."

"I'm so glad you shared that with me."

Buddy sat back in the chair and turned a page with the air of nobility. "I want to share the finer things in life with you, Robert."

"In that case, how about starting with Andi? I'll take Mondays, Wednesdays and Fridays. You can have Tuesdays, Thursdays and Saturdays. Sundays we rest."

"Not a chance, friend. Anyway, if memory serves, you have a girlfriend. She works at the Tap Room of the Holiday Inn."

"Her body works there ... but her mind is on vacation."

"We can't all be lucky enough to have that special mix of beauty and brains." Buddy paused to comb his hair and fix his collar. "Andi was just lucky enough to find me."

"Andi was lucky enough to what?!" Andi said as she walked into the lounge. She had heard only the tail end of the conversation. She tapped Buddy on the head, "Hi, Mutt."

She waved to Bob, "Hi, Jeff."

Buddy smiled, "Hi there, Art Lady."

"Now what were you fellas saying when I walked in?"

"Oh, your friend Rosen, here, was telling me how wonderful he is." Bob stood to rinse his cup in the sink. "You came in right before I threw up."

From the wall behind them, the popping sound of the intercom signaled a message. A voice spoke through the intercom. "Excuse me, this is Miss Rankin. Is Mr. Rosen in the lounge?"

Buddy looked at both of them and shook his head back and forth and mouthed No.

"I'm sorry, Miss Rankin, we couldn't hear you," Kevin said with a smile.

"Is that you, Mr. Kevin?"

"Yes it is."

"Well, Mr. Kevin, I was looking for Mr. Rosen. Have you seen him?"

Buddy again shook his head and gave a more exaggerated no this time.

"Why yes, I have," Bob said as Buddy stood up and started to go for his throat. "About ten minutes ago." Buddy relaxed.

"Do you know where he was headed?" Miss Rankin crackled through the system.

"No, Miss Rankin. I never know where Buddy is going." His body shook with quiet laughter.

"Yes. Well, if you see him, please tell him I would like to finish our discussion."

Andi and Bob looked at Buddy with raised eyebrows. "Certainly, Miss Rankin."

"Thank you, Mr. Kevin." There was the familiar popping sound signaling the end of the transmission.

"Naughty, naughty Mr. Rosen." Kevin teased.

"Awwww ... she loves me."

Andi said, "Hey, don't you have to get your kids at 11?"

"Yeah."

"Well, it's 11:05 now."

"Shit." He jumped up and ran past Miss Rankin, who was just stepping into the lounge.

"Mr. Rosen. I want to continue our discussion..." Miss Rankin called out to him as he yelled back a cursory, "Yes, ma'am."

"I found him," Bob Kevin said, pointing in Buddy's direction, smiling.

"What time is it?" Buddy asked as he cupped his ear.

"It's Home Movie Time!!" the class shouted together as they did every Wednesday at 11:30 a.m.

"15,984 Gold Stars for everyone," Buddy said as he set up his super 8 mm projector on the edge of the carpet. This was always a perfect way to bridge the time after activities and just before lunch. "Grab a seat. Popcorn is on the way."

Bodies dove around the projector as everyone jockeyed for position. Billy Gross and Valerie Saron were the "Ushers-of-the-day." They headed for the big oak cabinet that held plastic bowls and bags of pre-popped popcorn Buddy had bought that morning at Albertson's. Dutifully, Billy and Val served up the bowls to the hungry crowd.

"Let's see," Buddy said as he opened the movie case and pulled out a large discolored metal film container, "this one says: Christmas, 1957 New York City. What do you think? Should we show this one?"

"Yeah ... all right ..." came from every mouth in the classroom.

"Okay, now for the rules," said Buddy as he began to thread the film. "Please hold on to your ticket stubs, no talking, no snoring and no smoking in the theater."

"We don't smoke, Mr. Rosen," said John Stanley.

"That's good. We don't have any ashtrays. "

"Mr. Rosen ..." John smiled.

Buddy used home movies to get the kids thinking about story ideas. In the afternoon, they would talk about what they saw and create their own realities.

"I think this one ought to have some great shots of New York. Val, you get the lights and let's roll 'em." Buddy had absolutely no idea what was on this film or, for that matter, who the people were who took it. He got this film, like so many others he had, at the Flea Mart in Pinellas Park.

The familiar whir and clicks of the projector began as Buddy turned on the switch. He settled back in his director's chair as he watched the flickering images flash on the screen. He loved this time of the day as much as the kids did. Other people's home movies were his obsession.

> *Two tiny figures, one male and one female, walk quickly across the screen waving wildly at the camera as the Statue of Liberty jumps around in the background. The female figure points excitedly toward Lady Liberty and strikes the famous pose, pretending to hold the torch, looking serene. Her male companion bows regally and pretends to strike a match and*

light her torch. They both laugh and collapse into each other's arms.

Buddy watched intently and played mental detective. Who were these two on the screen? Obviously they weren't New Yorkers. Their first trip, no doubt. Were they married? Probably newlyweds. They were laughing far too much at their own jokes to be married more than a year.

The scene changes to Central Park. Three children run to the camera and then run in a circle playing tag. The younger of the three trips as she turns, gets up slowly and starts to cry. When she notices that no one is paying attention, her mouth opens even wider and the tears stream down her face. The female torch lady enters from the right and picks up the crying child cradling her head to her shoulder. The other children stop briefly to look and run off camera.

There goes the "one-year-married theory." Then again, maybe it isn't her baby. Or maybe the male figure was her brother. No, they look about as much alike as John Goodman and Madonna. In fact, they look like John Goodman and Madonna. He's not quite as fat.

Now the woman on the screen dances around in front of Macy's, loaded down with packages, looking like the old opening for "That Girl." The man is next to her looking depressed, showing an empty wallet to the camera. She kisses him on the cheek and winks. He motions to the cameraperson to stand where he is and walks toward the lens. The picture blurs and spins for a few seconds and then another female figure appears. The figure is an identical image of the first female. Twins. Except for the absence of a hat and a different dress, the second female is a clone.

Another piece to the puzzle. Is John Goodman married to the first Madonna or Madonna #2 ? Is Madonna #2 the mother of the little girl? What about the other children in the film?

"Mr. Rosen ... Mr. Rosen," Valerie was saying as she shook Buddy, "The bell rang five minutes ago." The other kids were giggling at the sight of him coming back to consciousness.

"Oh thanks, Val," he said, looking at his watch. "Lunchtime."

"You gonna eat that, Mr. Rosen?" Thomas Foley asked as he stuck his finger in Buddy's fat peanut butter and jelly sandwich he fixed that morning.

Buddy looked at Thomas and pushed the sandwich with the hole in the middle over to him. "I'm not too hungry. Here, you eat it."

"Thanks."

From behind a familiar voice whispered, "Hey, big boy, you wanna trade your banana for my pudding."

He looked up at Andi and said, "Nobody messes with my banana, sister. But I will make a deal with you for my Milk Duds."

"No thanks." Andi put her lunch down beside his and slipped next to him on the bench. "It's your banana or nothing."

"You know how guys feel about their bananas."

"Someday I'll tell you how girls feel about boys' bananas." Andi opened her lunch and took out her sandwich. She leaned over to look at Buddy's bag. "What else you got?"

"Let's see." Buddy opened his bag and pulled out a bag of Fritos and a Snickers candy bar. "Healthy stuff like this."

"I see." Andi picked up Buddy's bag and studied it. "You know, Buddy, I always wanted to ask you about this school bag."

"The R. Treader?" Buddy called it that because the name was stenciled on the side. "I bought it at the Salvation Army for 25 cents. I love this old thing. I think it's from the 1940s. The main reason I got it was because I wanted to meet R. Treader."

"Why?"

"Why? I don't know. Because I wanted to meet the guy who gave away a part of his childhood, I guess. Why did he give his school bag to the Salvation Army? It's like the home movies I find at flea markets and garage sales. I'm always amazed that people would let them go. It's like a part of your body. You might as well sell your arm."

"So you rescued it for Mr. Treader."

"Exactly," Buddy puffed out his chest.

"Did you ever find him?"

"Yep. I looked him up in the phone book. He was living in Clearwater."

"And ..."

"And I called him up to tell him I just bought his school bag. I asked if he remembered it."

"Did he?"

"He sure did. In fact, he had lost track of it. It seems his wife got rid of it in a box of old stuff she dumped off." Buddy stopped to take a bite of his banana. "I offered to give it back, but he said no. He wanted me to keep it. He said that he was just happy to hear it was being used. And especially by someone concerned about protecting his memories."

"That's sweet."

"Mmm, hmm," Buddy looked up. "Uh, oh, don't look now .... unhappy homemaker at twelve o'clock. "He was referring to the fast approaching Becky Sue Wright, third-grade teacher and teller of marital affairs. Her little feet made a clicking sound on the linoleum floor of the cafeteria like a toy machine gun.

She made it to their table in a fraction of a second. "Andi, I'm so glad I saw you," Becky Sue gushed as she put her face right between Buddy's and Andi's.

"Too late," Buddy said.

"What, Buddy?" Becky Sue asked.

"Nothing. I was just finishing a thought."

"Oh. Well anyway, Andi, you're not gonna believe what I just heard."

"Oh, yeah?" Andi answered.

"I was right. George Parker is involved with Sarah Bess. And Sarah Bess — the tramp! — is going through divorce number three as we speak. And that's not all. George has been going for counseling with Bunny. Can you imagine? She doesn't have a clue that he is cheating on her." She gestured to the far table where Sarah Bess was eating her lunch and reading a novel. "Look at her, as cool and calm as she can be while she just ruins poor Bunny's life."

"My, my," Buddy said sarcastically as Andi kicked him under the table.

"Well now, tell me, how are you lovebirds doing?"

"You mean you don't know?" Buddy leaned close to Becky Sue's ear.

"What?" Becky Sue strained to hear.

"Andi is three months pregnant with George Parker's baby." Andi almost spit up her food.

"Funny." Becky Sue said and trotted off to whisper into someone else's ear.

"Great, Buddy, now she will probably spread that rumor next." Andi said.

"It's about time. People need to know about your baby. I'm tired of keeping that our dirty little secret."

"You're terrible," Andi said as she got up to throw away her trash. "I don't know what I'm going to do with you."

"Meet me in the parking lot at 3."

Andi winked at Buddy over her shoulder as she looped her purse over her shoulder and walked out the cafeteria. Buddy watched her the whole time. He loved the way her body moved when she walked.

"Mr. Rosen." Fingers tapped on Buddy's shoulder. No need to look around, Buddy thought, he knew whose they were.

"Why, Miss Rankin, I was just going to come see you after lunch."

"I'll just bet you were." She was obviously at the end of her patience. Buddy decided not push her over the edge.

He looked at his watch. "It's nap time. After I tuck the kids in, I can come to your office."

"I wouldn't want to interrupt your nap, Mr. Rosen. I'll come to your room."

Buddy resisted the urge to offer her a pair of pajamas and a teddy bear. "Give me five minutes."

"That will be fine."

At naptime, the classroom was transformed into a military barracks. Kids in cots were lined up side by side. Each had a favorite blanket, animal or toy to sleep with. The lights were turned off and the shades pulled down low enough for only a little light to shine through.

Buddy's empty bunk was near the door.

He and Miss Rankin huddled together at his desk. In a whispered voice, Miss Rankin said, "Mr. Rosen, Buddy, I'll get right to the point. I have received a serious complaint from one of your parents."

Buddy sat straight in his chair and let out an audible sigh. "What kind of complaint?"

"This parent claims to have smelled liquor on your breath during a parent-teacher meeting."

She waited for a reaction. There was none.

"She was very disturbed by it. Quite frankly so was I."

Buddy leaned toward Miss Rankin so she could get a good whiff of his breath. "You believed her?"

"Well, I didn't want to believe it."

"— but, because I'm such an unorthodox character with questionable teaching methods, not to mention my past history of alcohol problems ..."

"Mr. Rosen," Miss Rankin raised her voice slightly and caused a few little heads to turn in her direction. She lowered her voice again to a whisper. "I did not say those things."

"I was making it easier for you."

Miss Rankin straightened her dress and looked him in the eye. "Have you been drinking during the day ... or not?"

"Does my answer make a difference?"

"Certainly."

"No, I haven't."

"Very well." Miss Rankin rose to her feet. "There is no need to address this issue again."

Buddy was stunned. "That's it? You believe me?" Buddy stammered. "I mean ... you don't want to ask me more questions?"

"No, Mr. Rosen." Miss Rankin turned to him. "Although I don't agree with your methods, your children are doing quite well and their skill levels are outstanding when they enter first grade. This other issue is closed. After talking to you, I am quite sure that there are no grounds for this complaint." She extended her hand to him.

"Thank you, really, thank you. That means a lot." Buddy shook hands and walked her to the door. He whispered in her ear. "Oh, listen, if that parent says anything about my personal relationships with small farm animals, don't believe her."

Miss Rankin stood straight and momentarily frowned.

Buddy winked.

The clock radio jarred Andi awake at 7:00 AM.

"Buddy."

Barely awake, Buddy made some undecipherable sounds. They were mixed with snoring and moaning.

"Buddy."

"Would you get it, Andi...?"

"Hmmpph," Andi mumbled as she stumbled over to the radio to hit the button. She pulled the pillow out from under his head and started smacking him with it.

"Hey, it's Saturday!" he said between swats.

"And this is the day you're supposed to pick up your daughter at the airport."

"It's only 7 o'clock. Her flight doesn't come in until noon."

"By the time you shave and shower, and I certainly hope you're planning to, it'll be close to eight. You've got time to buy Christina something special at the store."

"Aren't you coming with us?" he asked.

"No. She wants to spend time with her father. She doesn't want to spend time with her father's girlfriend."

"Does her father's girlfriend want to spend a little time with a slightly horny middle aged man this morning?"

"Go take a shower." They both laughed and wrestled in bed for a few minutes.

He pinned her. "Give up?"

She grabbed his crotch and said, "No. Do you? "

"Absolutely," Buddy kissed her passionately and unbuttoned his pajama top, which at the moment belonged to her.

She slipped down the bottoms, from his body. "Well what have we here, mister?"

"See ... somebody's up." He slid his thigh inside hers and kissed her again. Her mouth opened invitingly. He thrust his hips and immediately entered her.

He was lost in her smell and feel.

Buddy stepped into the shower. Andi followed behind grabbing him around the waist. She turned him so that the water fell on her back. "Stinker," Buddy said, "I thought this was my shower."

"Oh, I see. We are getting a little selfish are we?" Andi started to scrub and lather his back. "Maybe I need to get some of your share signs to put up in the shower."

"Funny."

"Where you taking Christina?"

"Maybe shopping." Maybe, nothing. He knew exactly where he was taking her. Buddy had this day planned for weeks. After he picked Chrissy up at the airport, they'd grab a bite to eat at his favorite seafood place. Then they'd hit the flea market for grins. And then the real surprise. He was going to present her with the keys to a new — well practically new — Honda. He couldn't wait to see her face. She had been talking about not having a car at school and what a drag it was.

"You don't seem too excited about seeing her."

"Sure, I'm excited. It's just, you know, I haven't seen her for a year." Chrissy's mom was picking up the tab for Princeton. She had done all right for herself. Between her catering business and new hubby's dental practice, they could well afford college tuition and such. Buddy just felt like a pauper when they talked about Chrissy. The car could be his contribution. He just hoped she liked it.

"Chrissy's a lucky girl." Her hands slipped around and down his thigh.

"Oh yeah? Why's that?" He suddenly had a raspiness to his voice.

"She's loved and adored by her daddy."

"I'm partial to daddy's girls." Buddy turned to wash her front.

Andi pulled away and turned to rinse.

"Hey, did I say something wrong?" Buddy tried to rub her shoulders. Andi stepped out of the shower and started to dry off.

Buddy rinsed quickly and turned off the water. "Andi, are you okay?"

There were tears running down the cheeks that were just dried. "I guess I'm just sentimental. Sorry I reacted that way."

"Could you pass me the towel?"

When Andi handed Buddy the towel he grabbed her in his arms tasting her slightly salty lips. "Thanks for not asking any more."

Buddy dug through his desk as Andi finished dressing. Christina's picture fell out of the bottom drawer. In the photo, she looked wondrously through a window, which reflected in one of her enormous hazel eyes. It was his favorite picture of her. She was two years old when he shot it. Even at two, Christina was always old beyond her years.

He dug deeper through the desk and found what he was looking for, an old album filled with wonderful memories. He turned to the page he shot of their trip to Washington, D.C. Chrissy was climbing on the dinosaur sculptures in the playground at the Smithsonian with about a dozen other kids. She looked so small. Actually, there were six pictures on the page, all identical: Chrissy climbing on the dinosaurs. "Very creative, Rosen," he thought to himself.

He'll never forget that trip. Janet and he walked Chrissy all day through the Smithsonian and she never got bored. She took it all in, absorbing it like a sponge. When they were about to leave the National Museum, Janet tried to take her hand.

Chrissy pulled her hand away and said, "Who are you, lady?"

Janet was stunned. She looked around embarrassed. "What are you talking about Chrissy? Just take my hand."

"I don't know you, Miss."

"Cut it out, Chrissy." Janet was clearly irritated. "These people are going to think that I'm not your mother."

"You're not my mother. My mother is French. You see, my name is Christina Michelle and I'm French, too."

Buddy burst into laughter and Janet picked her up and hustled her out the door. Chrissy looked surprised that she had caused a problem.

"Never do that again, Chrissy." Janet was livid. "We could have been arrested. Those people probably think I kidnapped you or something. And what are you laughing about, Buddy? This is your daughter. She's just like you, always joking around."

Buddy only laughed harder and so did Chrissy. She put her little chubby hand up to her mouth and started to giggle. Janet looked at both of them and finally burst into laughter herself. "Why did I ever marry you?"

"Because you're crazy about me," Buddy said.

"Either that or I'm just crazy."

"How about me?" Chrissy looked up at both, feeling left out.

"You?" Janet said. "I love you despite the fact that you are related to this guy."

Buddy kissed Janet. "...you pretend French lady, you."

They all hugged and laughed some more.

He turned to the Vienna pictures. There was a picture of Chrissy in Vienna with her hands on her hips, haggling with one of the flea market sellers. She stood there with a terrycloth outfit and bright pink plastic shoes.

Christina was a lot like Buddy. They were very close when she was younger. While they lived in Vienna, Buddy and Christina made weekly visits to the flea market at the center of town. He began to collect old brass irons engraved with the number of the brick size they held. Janet stopped counting after 50. He had an extensive collection of train watches and some of the most interesting toilet covers found in the city. She learned the barter trade quickly. Buddy used to burst into fits of laughter when his 4-year-old daughter stood toe to toe with an Austrian colporteur and asked, "Vas costa das?"

More Vienna pictures. They were skiing, watching a military parade, eating at a gasthaus and on a picnic in the country.

They did everything as a family. They traveled together; they played together; they were a perfect family unit. Buddy made sure of that. It was his obsession. He had a fear of things not working out. Just like they didn't work out for him when he was growing up.

Buddy put the album back. Next to the album, in the back of the drawer, was the carved wooden box that held his hash pipe and his stash so many years ago, it seemed. He stared out the window. Outside were two little children in bright bathing suits, hosing down each other as they played and screamed with delight.

Buddy was always a recreational drug user. Nothing really dangerous, just the popular drugs of choice in the 60's and 70's: grass, hash, an occasional mushroom or two, small amounts of coke. Janet knew this before they got married. She even participated in the early years ... before Christina.

Buddy had dreams back then. He was a musician ... not a great one but passable within his circle of friends, especially when they were stoned. He'd sit for hours playing guitar and writing songs about love and peace. Janet always supported him, telling him that his songs were filled with passion.

He joined a band — more like a trio of acoustic musicians — and sang in small clubs for awhile. He continued to teach during the day and play at night. The group had a small group of followers who would hang out and party late into the night.

Then Janet got pregnant.

Buddy's world changed. He wanted to do the right thing from the start. He quit the band, stopped smoking and focused solely on the baby's arrival. Janet was happy. Buddy was the perfect dad; it lasted until they left Vienna and moved to Baltimore for an administrative teaching position at a small private school.

Buddy didn't do well handling the pressure that went with his job. As admissions director, Buddy worked a full schedule and taught regular classes. He longed for the days that he could play music and smoke a joint or two. He placed a lot of unwarranted blame at Janet's feet.

Liquor replaced the drugs. Buddy had become more like his father. He hated it, but couldn't stop.

"Dammit, Janet, I just think we need to go back to Vienna. We were happy there."

"What's wrong with Baltimore? You have a great job, Chrissy's doing well in school ..."

"I need to get back to music. I could have had a career in music ..."

"So get into music here. I'm sure there are musicians here that you could play with."

"You don't get it ... it's just not Vienna."

"And you're not 24 years old and stoned every night, partying with your friends ..."

"Is THAT what you think I miss?"

"I don't know what you miss ... but you certainly haven't missed getting drunk every night I can attest to that. You know what I miss? I miss having a normal life — the one we had before you got this shitty new attitude."

"Really! So get the fuck out of the house and find yourself a normal life."

Janet bought two tickets back to New York, packed her bags and left Buddy a note.

Outside, the kids were running faster. Their voices were raised to a fevered pitch. The little boy who held the garden hose was running after the little girl. His foot got tangled in the hose and he did a nosedive on the sidewalk. His mother rushed around the front of the house when she heard the cries. She cradled him in her arms for a few minutes, then he jumped down and grabbed the hose again to resume the chase.

It was three years before Buddy saw Chrissy again. He quit drinking. Janet had remarried. She spoke to him by phone, but refused to meet him when he invited her to lunch. He wanted so much to see her ... for her to see him ... for her to be proud of him ... for her to know how sorry he was.

He took Christina instead.

Christina's eyes had that same wondrous look they had when she was two. The color had darkened slightly which made them more striking. She was leaving for college. Tears clung to the corners as she spoke to Buddy.

"I already know what you're going to say."

"What am I going to say?" Buddy asked.

"You're going to make some stupid joke about my hairdo just like you always did when I was younger."

"Boy, you see how wrong you are about me? My first words were going to be, 'You look more beautiful than ever.' Now would you comb your hair? It looks like you brushed it with an eggbeater."

"Oh, Daddy," Christina moaned, then threw her arms around him, "I missed you."

"How's your mom, Chrissy?" Buddy approached the subject head on.

"Rich and beautiful," answered Christina.

"Since when?" asked Buddy.

"Since she married that plastic surgeon," chimed Christina right on cue.

They broke into laughter. It was just like old times. Christina loved that old routine. Guaranteed to get a laugh. They used to always pull it on Christina's Aunt Susan. This is the first time they ever used it to describe Janet.

"Does she ever talk about me?" Buddy asked.

"Daddy," Christina looked at him with those eyes that could melt a thousand hearts.

"Seriously, does she ?"

"Sure she does."

"Well ... what does she say?"

"She told me that your smile could brighten the whole world," Christina said.

"The whole world?"

"Maybe New Jersey."

"She's still crazy about me, huh?"

Christina looked down at the floor. Suddenly, her expression changed. "Do you remember the day we left Baltimore?"

"How could I forget?" Buddy mumbled, "That was the lowest point in my life."

"Mom cried for so long that I thought she would die if she didn't stop. That night when she finally settled down, she came into my room and sat beside me on the bed. It was the first time I really remember feeling scared.

"Anyway, we talked for hours about the family and about starting over and then she told me something I've never forgotten ..." Christina paused.

"What was it?"

"She said I was a special person who had a special gift. It comes from within and there's no name for it. But everyone I meet will want to be close to it and, at the same time, will envy it. Use it wisely."

Buddy felt tears well up and tried to choke them back.

"Only one other person she knows has the same gift," Christina continued, "You, Daddy."

In the background Buddy could hear the phone ring. The answer machine clicked on and the voice on the other end replied:

"Daddy...it's me. I wanted to catch you before you went to the airport."

Buddy rushed over to pick up the phone.

"Guess what ? I'm not flying in. I'm driving in. Mom and Myles surprised me with a new Jeep, and a car phone ... Can you believe it?"

His hand froze on the receiver.

"... I just love it ... I'm on the road now ... I just passed Atlanta ... I'll be there by tomorrow morning ... I can't wait to see you ... love you ..."

Buddy felt Andi's arms circling around his neck.

The flea market was packed.

The lines of parked cars in the grassed-in parking lot were more common for a football game or an outdoor concert than a flea market on a typical weekend. Buddy and Andi had to find a spot on one of the last rows.

They had gotten there in mid-afternoon. Buddy really didn't want to go today, or so he said to Andi, but she convinced him to go with her. He soon forgot about Chrissy's call and started his search for valuable treasures.

"Buddy, look at this." Andi held a large brass pocket watch she picked up at one of the booths. It was a booth all to itself among the rows of hubcaps, used clothing, electronics, old pictures and the hundreds of tables filled with all types of memorabilia that filled the massive flea market.

There were no others like it around. The displays were very ornate.

"That's a German Staatbahn watch," Buddy said as he made his way past the racks of clothing and held the watch. "The train conductors used them in the early 1900's."

"Fifty dollars and it's yours," a voice from behind Buddy whispered hoarsely in his ear.

Buddy turned quickly to see a man dressed in a flannel shirt and khaki pants that had seen better days. The old man's eyes had a glint that time didn't erase. Unfortunately that was about all that had not been worn away with time. His hair had a look of electrified straw, badly in need of a comb. The stubble of his beard was erratic and traveled all the way down his flannel shirt. His teeth were yellowed and broken to match a nose that curved down the craggy face.

"What was that?" Buddy asked.

"That watch you been eyein'. You can have it for fifty," the old man answered.

"Fifty dollars is awful steep for this watch." Buddy countered.

"You know something about watches?" The old man looked closely at Buddy now.

"Something."

"Then you know that this here's a train conductor's watch. It's the finest of its kind, made in Germany and you know what they say about the Germans. They don't make nothin' that's not right to the second."

"Does it still work?"

"Yep. Still ticking since the turn of the century. Try it out."

Buddy picked up the watch and gently turned the stem back and forth between his thumb and forefinger. He placed it to his ear and heard the familiar ticking.

"You're a collector, ain't you?" the old man asked.

"Is it that obvious?" Buddy asked.

"Collectors got a certain look. The way you picked up that watch and caressed it like it was a beautiful woman. Nothing personal, ma'am."

Andi winked, "I'm sure you meant it as a compliment ... to the watch."

"And to your beauty, too, of course," the old man said.

"I'll give you thirty five for it, "Buddy said.

"I could never part with it for less than forty five."

"Forty."

"Sold."

Buddy smiled.

"Hey, collector. I think you're gonna like this too." Andi had drifted over to the rear of the booth and was looking at something sitting on the ground.

"Interested in movies, are we?" The old man said as Buddy paid for the watch.

Buddy's interest was piqued. He followed the old man to where Andi stood. There sat a box opened on the top. A rusty film canister sat among newspapers that were balled up. Buddy knelt closer and removed the newspapers to examine the contents. He spied an old clock and camera equipment and as he lifted up a layer of papers he caught a glimpse of more of the treasure that he never could resist.

"Make me an offer," the old man said.

"For the box?" Buddy asked.

"Yeah, sure, for the whole thing."

"Well, I don't know what all is in there or what it's worth."

"Neither do I," said the old man. "That is, I don't know everything that's in there. I do know the camera doesn't work, but the clock does. The rest is a bunch of trash as far as I'm concerned."

Andi interrupted, "Buddy, the clock would be nice on the fireplace."

"Will you take twenty bucks?" asked Buddy.

"Twenty bucks! You gotta be kidding."

"What will you take for the box?"

"How about fifty?"

Buddy quickly checked his finances and looked at the box one more time. "All I've got is thirty."

"Okay, call me a sucker. I know I shouldn't do it. There will probably be someone here right after you leave offerin' me a hundred bucks. But I got a soft spot for collectors. Gimme your lousy thirty."

The old man lifted the box into Buddy's arms and pocketed the ten and the twenty Buddy had in his hand. "Enjoy."

"Thanks."

Buddy glanced down at the top of the box just briefly enough to read A.R. on the label.

Buddy started to ask the old man a question but he had already started to talk to another customer. Just at that moment, he turned to look at Buddy over his shoulder. And he winked.

Buddy couldn't wait to open his newfound treasure.

He tried to act interested in Andi's conversation at dinner, but all he could think about was whipping out the projector and putting the films on. Andi was telling him that she had to counsel a girlfriend who just got dumped by her boyfriend, or maybe her girlfriend, Buddy couldn't remember.

He helped clear the table as Andi washed the dishes.

"You haven't listened to one word I've said, have you?" Andi put down a dish and looked in his direction.

"Sure, I did. Let's see ... you just said that Karen was in such distress over Frank's moodiness that she was considering a divorce but instead opted for a temporary separation followed by years of counseling leading to certain reconciliation and no doubt continued verbal abuse." Buddy took a deep breath.

"Yeah. I should give you some verbal abuse."

"I love it when you talk dirty." Buddy pulled her to him and planted a big kiss on her lips.

She smiled at him and patted his butt. "Okay. Go look at your films. I'm leaving anyway."

"You mean ..."

"Yes. I am going to Denise's house — not Karen's — to talk about Aldo, her son. Not Frank, her husband — and help her find a treatment center for his psychological problems."

"That was going to be my second guess."

"Sure, Mr. Sensitivity." Andi grabbed her keys and put them in her pocket. She headed for the door. "Bye, now. Don't wait up."

Buddy ripped through the box of films and camera parts like a man possessed.

The reels were enclosed in large, rusty canisters without labels and some were just reels without the canisters. He looked at each one, studying them, trying to imagine the owner. It was a little game he played that gave him great pleasure. This owner was a pretty active shooter, he thought, based on the volume in the box. The camera parts were pretty extensive, as well. The owner was a hobbyist much like his father, he thought, there were camera parts in here that resembled some he grew up with.

He set up the screen, opened one of the canisters and looped the film through the projector. He flipped the switch and settled into his favorite movie chair as the first trail of numbers flew by.

... 8 ... 7... 5 ... 3... The frame blurs as the camera swerves and finally focuses on a little girl sitting at a table covered with a paper tablecloth and decorated with party favors. She waves and says something to the cameraman. She points to the right as the camera turns in that direction and catches another girl with thousand freckles and glasses with the rims winged on the side. She also waves, a little shy wave, and smiles a slightly frightened smile. The camera moves again and there is another little face smiling and this one has no sign of shyness. The hands wave wildly and the mouth opens wide ...

The phone rang on the table next to Buddy. He picked up the receiver, "Hello?"

"Hi, Daddy," Christina said on the other end of the phone.

"Who's this?"

"It's your worst nightmare."

"Oh. Hi, Chrissy."

"Are you busy?"

"Nope, just watching a movie."

... a birthday cake held by a woman with short curly hair blurs past ...

"Did you get my message?"

"Sure, honey. I was sorry you couldn't make it today."

... the candles leave a long trail of light...

"Me too."

...they all crowd in and sing happy birthday...

"How's the car?"

... the birthday girl takes a deep breath and blows out only one candle. The rest of them stand back up defiantly. Everyone laughs hysterically as she tries one more time...

"Just great. It handles well on the road. I stopped in Tallahassee for the night."

"You at a hotel?"

"Yes. At the Holiday Inn. The number's 555-1002. Room 234."

... from the right of the picture frame the short curly haired woman moves in close and hugs the birthday girl cheek to cheek. They both smile at the camera ...

Buddy focused on the face and temporarily lost track of the conversation.

"Anyway, Dad, I'll probably get there in the morning. I'll come right to the house."

He knew that face.

"... Oh, Dad? Earth to Dad. Did you hear what I said?"

"... Yes, honey. I'll be here. I can't wait to see you."

"I can't wait to see you either. Dad ... There is one other thing that might catch you by surprise: I got my hair cut. It's pretty short."

... the curly-haired woman motions to the camera man to give her the camera and the image in the camera blurs and swings 180 degrees ...

Buddy strained to refocus on the screen as it cleared.

"Oh, my God," Buddy mumbled into the receiver.

"Well it's not that short ..."

"... Gotta go, honey, I'll see you tomorrow."

"Daddy?"

Buddy had dropped the phone and was staring at the image on the screen. It couldn't be, he thought to himself. No, it must just be a coincidence.

... everyone was eating birthday cake while the birthday girl sat in the middle opening a mound of brightly colored presents and reading the cards with Happy Birthday Audrey on them...

He threw back his chair and made his way to the hall closet. Sliding back the door, Buddy reached up for the overflowing cardboard box that held hundreds of loose photos and stuff.

His mind began racing and his heart pounded against his chest, vibrating his teeth with each beat.

The box overturned on top of him, spilling out the contents over the floor. Buddy was like a madman, diving into the scattered pile of pictures.

"There it is," Buddy said aloud. Under the mess, he spotted a corner of a picture. It was the only photo left of his mom and dad. Buddy had hidden the picture when he went to live with his Aunt Selma. The picture was small and wrinkled and faded, but he could make out the faces.

He ran back to the living room and reversed the film until he saw the image he was looking for:

... Now the cameraman appeared. He takes off his sunglasses ...

His heart beat so hard it seemed to break through his chest. The room got very hot. The cameraman was HIS FATHER. How could it be? And the curly haired woman? Yes, it was HIS MOTHER.

"Audrey ... Audrey Jennings ... This is her party." Buddy thought aloud as he tried to make some sense of it all. "This is crazy. These are my home movies."

... Audrey was thanking everyone and shaking hands down a long line of party guests. There, right at the end of the line was Buddy with a big smile...

Buddy swallowed hard.

His Dad's trademark shot was the line of guests shaking hands. He used to do that at all functions, even family events. It was so stupid. Everyone used to make fun of him. But he didn't care. "It looks great in the camera," he used to say.

Buddy tore through the box looking for answers. There was a framed picture at the bottom of the box. It was covered with a light film of dust. He wiped the glass. His hands trembled as he looked at the family portrait. It was a studio picture of Buddy and his mom and dad posed with their heads together.

"This can't be happening. No. It's not real. It's a horrible joke. That old guy who sold this to me. Gotta find out where he got these."

He opened the next canister. The other had finished rewinding so he snapped it off the spindle and replaced it with the one he held in his hand. He threaded it carefully, and started the switch.

... Lines of scratches through the first shots make it hard to determine what is in the frame. As it clears there is a shot of a boat and a dock. The camera studies the boat from bow to stern. It comes to rest on the name "Abe's Fare Maiden"...

Buddy smiled. Most people would think that Abe made a grammatical error ... not so. His father was a taxi driver from New York before he moved to Florida. He met his future bride when she was his passenger. The boat was named for her.

... the picture jumps to the swells of the waves taken from the boat. There is Buddy with a fishing rod, waving at the camera and looking over the bow to see if he hooked anything. Then there is a shot of his dad reeling one in. He yells over his shoulder to Buddy. Buddy runs over with a net as his dad motions with his head to get the fish as he brings it up ...

He looked away for a second, remembering this trip too well.

... Buddy reaches down and drops the net overboard. His dad is furious. He throws his rod down in a gesture of complete frustration and slaps Buddy on the side of the head. He screams something else and then looks in the camera shrugging his shoulders and waving his hands to stop the film...

His head was still turned away when he heard the slap of the film hitting the base as it spun around. He opened the next film canister. Buddy moved a little more slowly now. He was getting more and more anxious with each new discovery. He pulled the last reel off without rewinding and switched the reels so that the top reel became the take-up reel. He threaded it carefully.

> *... Closeup of a kid dressed as a bunny, sitting on the corner squinting up to the camera facing the sun. The costume is a cheap flimsy one with a jacket worn over it. The bunny points down the street and the camera swings sharply in that direction. There are motorcycles headed toward the camera. Mardi Gras signs adorn the street lights ...*

Buddy stopped the film and ran to the desk pulling out pen and paper. He turned the projector on ...

> *... More costumes. A ballerina with a black mask covering her eyes. Two older folks sitting in lawn chairs behind the kids waiting for the parade. They look at the camera. Both had shawls around their legs ...*

Buddy didn't remember a trip to New Orleans for Mardi Gras. Maybe this is one that his parents took without him. He took notes about what he saw for a reference sheet to put in the canister ...

> *... The older lady holds up a sign that says "throw me something, Mister." They all wave and laugh. The older man grabs the sign and hands it to the little ballerina to hold. The parade comes down St. Charles Ave. and "mom"runs out*

to the street to beg for beads and trinkets. She shows the camera handfuls of junk she caught...

"St. Charles Avenue ... parade," Buddy wrote as the film continued. He thought to himself, "I don't know any of these people. What is this film about?"

... The kids fall asleep with their heads together. The couple motions to the cameraman to come closer. No, to join them. The older gentleman walks toward the camera and gestures to the cameraman to have a seat and he would take the picture. The camera swings around and the cameraman joins the others. He waves and then shakes hands and walks toward the camera...

Buddy took a deep breath and rewound that scene.

... The camera swings around and the cameraman joins the others. He waves and then shakes hands and walks toward the camera ...

He did it again.

... The camera swings around and the cameraman joins the others. He waves and then shakes hands and walks toward the camera ...

Buddy looked incredulously at the face and then down at the portrait on his lap. It was him. He looked more than 10 years older but it was definitely his dad. The Mardi Gras sign was dated 1974. Fourteen years after ... his parents' death.

Buddy put his hands over his eyes.

... The film stopped frozen between frames. Dark circles grew over the face of Buddy's dad ...

The familiar smell of burning celluloid took over the room.

Buddy's wasn't looking at the screen anymore. He stared at the picture on his lap.

God ... he might still be alive ... his mom might too ... somewhere.

He pulled the plug.

Lightning flashes. Buddy races on his bike and pedals quickly laughing and pointing as he passes Max. Suddenly, Max is under the tires of a passing car, screaming. His bike is crushed. More lightning . Everything turns upside down, then just blackness ...

"Daddy? Daddy, are you all right?" Chrissy was standing over him as he opened his eyes. Buddy looked down at his clothes and realized he slept where he sat, in the living room. He was wet with his own sweat. Buddy saw the framed photo still sitting on his lap and the projector unplugged. He blinked the sweat from his brow.

The nightmares were back.

"Chrissy," Buddy bolted upright. The photo flew off his lap and hit the floor. The glass shattered on impact. He bent down and picked up the frame with the cracked glass in it and placed it next to the projector. He hugged her tight.

"You are soaking wet."

"When did you get here? ... How was the drive? ... Sorry ... I had a bad night, honey. Here ... sit, sit."

Buddy cleaned off a chair and led her to it.

"The dreams are back, huh?" Chrissy said.

Buddy collapsed back into his chair. "Yes."

"I was worried about you after we talked on the phone," Christina picked up the phone receiver from the floor and replaced it in the cradle.

"Don't worry, Chrissy, it just gives you wrinkles."

"What were you watching last night?" Christina looked at all the film cases.

"Movies ... old movies of your grandparents."

"Papa and Grandma?"

"No, no. My parents, the grandparents that you never knew." Buddy picked up a reel and looked at a film strip in the light as if he could see an image.

"I thought you didn't have any movies of them."

"I don't. I mean I didn't. I got these at the flea market." Buddy paused and looked closely at Christina, "One was made 14 years after they died and my dad was in it."

"What?"

"Chrissy, I know it sounds impossible to believe. I still don't quite believe it myself. But, he was there on the screen in a different city."

"A different city?"

"Yes, New Orleans. There's lots more. I wrote down some notes." Christina just sat with her mouth open. "Tell you what, you unpack and I'll get dressed. Then we'll try to figure this out together. Deal?"

"Okay." Christina was still in shock. "Is this a joke you're playing on me?"

"I wish this was a joke, honey. But, unless someone is playing one on me, it looks like your grandparents either didn't die in the boat accident after all or they have remarkable body doubles somewhere." Buddy went to the bedroom to dress.

Chrissy had a knot in her stomach. She picked up the reels of films and dropped them into the cardboard box. She found an envelope taped to the inside of the lid that had gone unnoticed by Buddy. She lifted off the envelope and turned to put it on the table.

The shattered picture still lay on the table, the glass distorting the images below. Christina picked it up, too. She carried it to the garbage can in the kitchen and brushed away the glass shards. The picture lifted up out of the frame and almost fell into the trash as well. Christina rescued it in time but dropped the frame and the envelope into the trash before she could catch it. She reached in to grab it. Her hand felt the slice of a big piece of glass before she could fish it out. She pulled back in pain and gave out a small scream.

Buddy rushed in to see what happened. "Chrissy, are you all right?"

"Yeah. It was a stupid accident. Sorry, Dad, I'll clean up your floor." Christina looked at the blood drops that splattered across the floor as she pulled her hand over the sink. "I cut myself on the broken glass pieces from the picture frame."

"Hold still, I'll just run some water over it and take a look." Buddy washed the cut and examined her hand. It seemed to be a bad cut but not deep enough for stitches. "You should know by now that cleaning up Buddy Rosen's messes is dangerous duty."

"I survived."

"You got lucky." Buddy hugged his daughter. "So did I."

Buddy looked over at the picture of his mom and dad. He realized at that moment how much Christina resembled his mother. "God, you look so much like her."

Christina studied the picture that sat on the counter. "What was she like?"

Buddy wrapped Christina's hand in a piece of gauze that he took from the bottom drawer. "I remember that she was very beautiful. She modeled in New York when she was younger."

"Is that where she was from?"

"No. She was from Birmingham, Alabama. Her father ran a print shop in town."

Buddy's memories of childhood conversations started coming back: "I remember her telling me once how much she hated Alabama and how her father was a pretty cold and heartless kinda guy who just worked all the time and didn't have much to do with her, I guess. Her mother was a timid woman who was always sickly. Anyway, on the day she finished high school she packed her bags and left for New York. She never went back."

"Is that where she met Grandpa Abe?"

Buddy smiled, "He was the very first person she met when she got to New York. They used to tell the story over and over. Abe Rosen picked up Frances Eliot outside of Grand Central Station. Abe was a 29-year-old cab driver and took one look at this scared, skinny kid with a heavy Alabama accent and fell in love. It was just like 'Bridget loves Bernie:' The Jewish New Yorker meets The Shiksah from the South."

"How romantic."

"It was all they had, for a while. Abe's income didn't go too far. Frances got part-time modeling jobs and worked some at a cocktail lounge as a 'hostess.' They kinda bounced around for a while ..."

Christina interrupted, "I thought Grandpa Abe was in the motel business."

"He was, eventually. You see, one night, this passenger in his cab started to have chest pains. He told Abe he needed to get to a hospital ASAP. Abe hit the gas, but the traffic was horrible and the pains got worse. The guy started to die in the cab. Abe pulled over and gave him CPR ... saved his life. Turns out this guy was a multimillionaire from Florida and gave Abe a start at a new life managing a piece of property in St. Petersburg. When he died ... he left the motel to Abe."

"The Palms Motel."

Buddy smiled at Christina. "That's the place."

"Knock, knock." Andi leaned into the kitchen. She was holding a large bouquet of flowers in one hand and a bottle of wine in the other. "The door was open so I just ..."

Buddy jumped up and gave Andi a hug. "Come in, come in and meet the family, Andi."

"Special Delivery for Ms. Christina Rosen." Andi held out the gifts.

Christina accepted them and gushed. "Oh, wow! These are gorgeous. Thank you so much." She looked to Buddy for an introduction.

"Chrissy this is Andi Fenimore. Andi and I are, um ..."

"Good friends," Andi saved him from further embarrassment. "In addition to being a good friend, I'm also the art teacher at Coquina Preparatory."

"It's very nice to meet you." Christina took the flowers to the sink to put them in the water.

"Dad, I knew you had good taste."

"Well, honey you should really give Andi credit. She really picked these out."

"I'm not talking about the flowers," Christina winked at Andi.

"Thanks, Chrissy." Andi smiled. "I know how happy your father is that you are here. He even had to put up with me as a substitute at the flea market yesterday."

"The flea market." Buddy suddenly remembered the box of films. "We've got to go back there today."

"Buddy you've got lots of time for that. Let Chrissy relax. Besides we just went there yesterday."

"Exactly, I'll explain in the car."

The only person at the flea market was Sid Portland, the assistant manager. He was talking to Buddy through the mesh window that separated the small office from the rest of the world.

"It ain't open today. I told you, we got some renovatin' going on. Come back next weekend."

Buddy insisted: "I just want to ask you a few questions about a vendor."

"Listen, Mister, we ain't responsible for no problems you might have had with a vendor. We only provide space. You're gonna have to talk to him in person." Portland started to close the wooden door that sealed the window.

"No. Wait. I haven't had a problem with a vendor. I just want to talk to one, that's all."

"Fine. Come back next weekend."

Chrissy had an idea. "Excuse me, sir, my father is really looking for vendor information about renting some space for next weekend. One of your vendors was selling the type of merchandise that we were interested in."

Sid Portland looked over the trio. His eyes shifted from Andi to Chrissy and finally to Buddy. "Well, why didn't you say so? Come on in."

He stood up to open the door at the rear of the building. They were ushered into the small office. Buddy hugged Chrissy and whispered, "Aren't you the cagey one!"

Portland shifted his huge frame behind the small wooden desk that held twice its weight in paper. "Okay, I've got prime space if you want to take it for 6 months at $50 a shot or $1,200 lump. It's located right here." Portland pointed to a space on the large map of the grounds that hung by a wire behind his desk.

Buddy looked closely at the map and tried to read all the vendors names. "Where is the front entrance in relation to that spot?"

Portland moved some of the stacks of papers off his desk. Somehow in that mass of trash he found what he was looking for. "Here. This'll help you get your bearings. This is our locator key. The red lane is in the front. Then you have the green and yellow sections on the north and south. White areas and orange areas flank east and west." He turned the plastic card over. "Now here's where you can tell who's who. The numbers tell what kind of vendors they are. For example, all the 1000's are the clothing guys, 2000's are the jewelry vendors, 3000's are the antiques, etcetera. You understand?"

"Yes. I think so."

"Mr. Portland, which group of numbers sell cameras and watches?" Chrissy chimed in as Buddy smiled. She read his mind.

"Those could be the 2000's for jewelry." Portland looked on the list. "but mostly in the 7000's, 'cause they's mechanical and antique people. Is that what you folks sell?"

"That's what we're interested in." Buddy added. "Do you have lots of, um, 7000's in the mart?"

"Depends on the weekend. Yesterday, we had quite many."

"We noticed one in this area over here," Buddy said as he pointed to the western part of the map.

"That'd be real unusual, I'd say."

"Why is that?" Andi asked.

"Because that's an area we don't lease to 7000's or any other thousands for that matter. It's what we call a traffic lane. We gotta keep it clear for fire code. You must have seen them in another spot."

"I don't think so." Buddy said. "I remember a booth with a big bear that was right next to it." He pointed just south of the booth.

"That'd be the Simpson's booth. No missing it. They sell outdoor clothing and stuff. But it couldn't be there." Portland crossed his arms and looked at Buddy. "It's the last one in the section. Unless ..." Portland turned back to the map, "Well, this here section does attract some bloodsuckers."

"Bloodsuckers?" Andi asked.

"Yeah, you know, like vendors without a license, suckin' up all the business. They sneak in sometimes in the rush and set up portable booths and sell out quick. They're tricky."

"Thank you, Mr. Portland." Buddy reached out and shook hands. "We'll let you know about our decision."

Buddy's dining room table was covered with pieces of paper, film canisters and two boxes of half-eaten pizzas. Buddy walked around the room waving a piece of pizza with pepperoni and mushroom in the direction of Andi and Chrissy.

"So, what do we have? A box of movies starring my parents who really died 14 years before they were filmed, their new family and friends who I don't even know, living in a city I've never been to. To top it off, they were sold by a grisly old bloodsucker at the flea market who no one knows. I'd say we're making progress, wouldn't you?"

"There's got to be some rational explanation for this," Andi answered as she attempted to clean up some of the clutter.

"I'm sure there is, Andi. I bet we'll all have a good laugh when we find out that my mom and dad were really double agents using super 8mm movies as their only means of communication."

Chrissy hugged him. "You've been reading those comic books again, haven't you Daddy?"

"I told you they'd come in handy some day."

Suddenly Chrissy had a thought. "Double agents."

"What?"

"Double agents. You said double agents."

"Don't forget coded home movies."

"Seriously, Daddy." Chrissy picked up a pencil and started to write. "What if they were living double lives? Abe might have had a whole different family living in another city."

"Abe had a parallel life? I don't think so. He could barely handle the life he made ... and he never really left the motel. Frances on the other hand would have welcomed some peace and quiet. She would have packed his bags."

"Well ... maybe. It's a possibility."

"How about this ... Abe has a body double in New Orleans who he hired to create a real family that did stuff like eat dinner together instead of drink it."

"Sorry ..." Buddy grabbed a beer from the refrigerator. "I need some air. Andi, hand me the garbage can, will ya? I might as well do something useful like take out the trash."

Andi picked up the trashcan and handed it to Buddy, who was halfway out the door when Chrissy grabbed it from him. "Wait ... don't do that. There's something in there. "

"Did you lose a finger or something?"

"No." Chrissy gingerly pinched out the envelope that had a single drop of blood — her blood — on it. "This! It was taped inside the box and I accidentally dropped it when I was cleaning up the glass."

She handed it to Buddy, who carefully opened the flap. Inside was a key with a piece of cardboard attached. On one side there was a number:

BOX 125639.

The other side had an address:
Beach Bank and Trust
100 Shore Parkway
St. Petersburg 33704

"Beach Bank and Trust ... that's been gone a long time. It's changed hands a few times ... Bank of St. Petersburg

Beach is there now," Buddy said. "Tell you what. I will check this out while you both write a list of other theories. Like ... teleportation, cryogenetics, body doubles ..."

"Oh ... go make a withdrawal." Chrissy said.

The parking lot of The Bank of St. Petersburg Beach was empty.

Buddy turned off the ignition and sat motionless. Thoughts of Abe and Frances were swimming through his head. What if this key unlocked secrets that were locked away for years? Hadn't he finally come to grips with his childhood nightmares? Not really. The nightmares still haunted him. What he found might release him — or it might make the nightmares worse.

"Need some help?" The bank security guard knocked on the outside of Buddy's window and looked into his car from above.

"What?" Buddy nearly jumped out of his skin. "No. No. I'm fine, " he said as he rolled down the window. "Wasn't sure if you were open today."

"Oh yeah, we're open. Just slow on the weekend," the guard said.

"Okay, thank you." He opened the door and practically sprinted inside, leaving the guard 20 steps behind.

At the security desk another guard took him down to the vault area where a bank official greeted him, checked his identification and took him to the box. "We still see these keys from the old boxes from Beach Bank. Got new ones if you're interested."

"No, that's okay. I'll stick with the old one," Buddy smiled and answered.

The long metal box was handed to Buddy to examine in one of the private vault rooms. He unlocked it with his key in the solitude of a small cubicle.

Buddy took a deep breath and opened the lid with a great flourish. He half expected a spirit to float out with his parents' faces. No ghosts — yet.

He looked over the contents for a few minutes before touching anything. It was almost as if Buddy had unlocked a sacred shrine that carried with it some ancient curse if touched.

The first thing that caught his eye was a black velvet pouch. He untied the string that held it together. The covering fell open to reveal four exquisite diamond necklaces with matching earrings and three large diamond and sapphire rings. His eyes were as big as saucers. He quickly folded the velvet over the jewelry and looked nervously around as if someone were watching his every move.

He pulled out a notebook. Ledger sheets from The Palms Motel stuck out of its cover. There were lots of names listed in, what appeared to be, alphabetical order. Adams, George ... Bennett, Senator James ... Brandt, Jayne ... Cabrera, John ... It was filled with old baby pictures, family photos, diplomas, certificates and there were news clippings. One of the clips had the headline: SISTERS MURDERED AT PALMS. It was a large article that took up most of the front page of the Times. There was a picture of the motel and the crowd of bystanders outside. Another picture showed a man handcuffed between two policemen, with a caption below: Jennings is arrested outside the Palms. The other clip showed a picture of a wrecked boat beached on the shore. Above the picture read: Beach couple presumed dead. Two picture inserts of Abe and Frances Rosen were to the right of the boat.

"The bodies," Buddy said aloud. "I remember ... They never recovered the bodies."

Under the notebook was a diary that belonged to Frances. Buddy felt a rush of excitement as he picked up the diary. He flipped through the pages quickly. The missing pieces to the puzzle must be here.

At the bottom of the box was a small jewelry box. Buddy opened the box and saw the gem-encrusted ring with the letters SOB.

"I'll be damned ... the SOBs ... haven't thought about them in years."

Buddy looked at his watch. He put everything in the briefcase he brought. He handed the safety deposit box back to the bank guard, who escorted him to the door.

He didn't notice the shadowy figure reading the newspaper in a nearby car.

Buddy turned down Beach Road.

He passed Save the Beaches Foundation and pulled into The Palms Hotel next door. Even though the new structure maintained the feel of the original, the old motel had been remodeled and updated dramatically. To Buddy, it had none of the charm, or the bad memories. Buddy stepped out of the car and walked in the front door. He waved to the concierge, a thirty-something South American beauty named Margarita Martinez, as he passed through the lobby lined with parrots in ceiling high cages and surrounding a fountain in the center.

"Hey, Buddy." Margarita said with a wink.

Buddy walked up to her desk. "Margarita, where is that lowlife husband of yours?"

Margarita leaned over and whispered, "Probably in his office doing his secretary."

"Shame, shame, shame. If I were Ramon and you were my wife ... I'd never leave the house. "

Ramon Martinez, hotel manager and husband of Margarita, walked up next to her. "Just have her home by midnight."

"Ramon, you're a lucky guy." They exchange handshakes as Buddy bends Ramon's ear. "Hey, you got a few minutes?"

"Sure. You want to use the office?"

"As long as your secretary doesn't mind." Buddy winked at Margarita.

She blew him a kiss.

Buddy walked around the office looking at Ramon's bookshelves and awards. He picked up a gavel made out of seashells. It sat in front of a wooden base engraved with: "Sons of Beaches President Ramon Martinez." The logo was identical to the ring that Buddy found in the jewelry case.

"Are you still president?" Buddy asked.

"Two more months. Hey, by the way, when are you gonna come back to our meetings? Last one you made was right after Kennedy was shot."

"Not true. It was during the Nixon administration." Buddy looked out the window and noticed the back of the Foundation building. "Caught you on TV this morning."

"Oh yeah? I missed it. How did I do?"

"You were passionate, man. I wanted to go out, head to the beach and start dredging myself."

Ramon laughed.

Buddy's expression changed as he looked around the room again. "I remember this office, you know? Big Abe sat right where you're sitting now."

He walked to the opposite side. "Funny, the stuff you remember and the stuff you forget."

Buddy looked back and forth. "Anyway ... I came to ask a favor. Did you ever keep stuff from the old days?"

"What stuff?"

"Stuff like old guest registers, pictures, mementos ... "

"How old?"

"Back when my dad had the motel."

"Nope. We don't have anything more than about ten years old. Buddy, why are you thinking about that stuff now?"

Buddy shrugged his shoulders. "Ahh. Just old ghosts, you know? They show up sometimes." Buddy opened his briefcase and pulled out the ring. "Like Abe's ring. I just ... found it."

Suddenly, Buddy remembered something. "Could have sworn he was wearing it when he ... well ... you know ... he never took that thing off."

Ramon's intercom beeped once. "Yeah?"

"It's noon, Ramon." Lydia's voice was heard on the speaker.

"Thanks, Lydia."

He looked up at Buddy. Ramon got out of his chair and took Buddy by the arm.

"Come with me."

"What? Where are we going?"

Ramon lead him out the door. "To have lunch."

"You and me?"

"And a few of your favorite Ghostbusters."

The big banner was draped across the entrance of the Palms Ballroom with S.O.B. sewn in white letters across a gold-and-blue velvet backing. The Sons of Beaches emblem was centered below.

A bespectacled bald-headed man was smiling up at Buddy from behind the table of neatly arranged badges and membership check lists. The bald-headed man's hand extended under Buddy's nose. "Hank Cockburn." Hank was very matter of fact. "Don't think I've had the pleasure."

Buddy shook his hand. "Buddy Rosen."

Hank scanned the badges. "Well ... let's see ... I can't seem to find your name."

"Really? Well, Hank, I'm sorry ... must be in the wrong place ..."

Buddy started to turn around. Ramon stopped him and turned him back to the table.

"It's okay, Hank. He's with me. Last meeting he attended was when you had hair."

Hank smiled and pointed a "finger gun" at Buddy. "That was a long time ago, son."

Buddy pointed back as he and Ramon walked toward the front. Buddy whispered, "I'll get you for this ... you ... Son of a BEACH!"

"Here, sit." Ramon pulled out a chair. Buddy waved at the members circled around the table. They all waved back.

"I'll be back ... gotta get this thing started."Ramon stepped up to the podium, tapped the microphone a few times and called the meeting to order. "All right ... all right ... settle down you drunken SOBs. Let's get started."

Carl Johnson yelled out, "What's the hurry, Ray? Margarita waiting in the honeymoon suite?"

Laughter broke from the crowd.

"You should know about hurrying, Carl." Stanley Young snickered, "Shirley told me that's the way you always do it at home."

More laughter.

"Very funny, guys. Stanley, since you were the last to speak, why don't you do the invocation?"

Stanley stood up and tried to look solemn. "Sure Ray ... okay ... let us pray. God, please bless this food we are about to eat today and bless our humble homes that sit on your beautiful beaches — maybe you can strike down some of those bastards who oppose the referendum."

"Amen!" said Ramon and the crowd. "Thanks, Stanley. Okay, let's eat."

Buddy opened his silverware as the old man sitting to his right peered over his half glasses in Buddy's direction. "Buddy? Is that you, son? Haven't seen you in years."

Buddy shook his hand. "Hey, Mr. Sweeney. You doin' okay?"

"Aah, could be better. Robbing me blind at the store." Sweeney leaned in closer. "Coloreds ... you know? What are ya gonna do? Gotta have workers."Sweeney stopped to take a big mouthful of green beans. Buddy looked across the table at Calvin Robinson, the black attorney who caught his eye. Buddy raised his eyebrows as Calvin smiled and shook his head ... as if to say "heard it before."

Sweeney continued. "What about you, still working up north?"

"No, teaching school right here."

"Smart kids?"

"Well, they're all potty-trained."

Sweeney nodded. "Good. You're lucky."

At the podium again, Ramon got everyone's attention. "Okay. Everybody can keep eating while I go on with announcements." Ramon shuffled through his papers to find what he was looking for. He cleared his throat. "Let's see. Anyone interested in the softball tournament this Saturday, see Davey. We need the players. Davey said we're down three ... so please guys ... if you can do it, we need you ... also ... George Banks asks that I announce the passing of two of our dear friends and founding members of the SOB organization this past month. Timothy Hassford, 66, of Toledo, Ohio, died in a fatal car accident and Benjamin Moskovitz, 68, of Newark, New Jersey, died peacefully at home."

Buddy listened intently and then jotted a note in his pocket notebook.

Ramon looked over at Buddy. "Buddy Rosen, would you please come up?" Buddy hesitatingly stood and made his way to the podium, embarrassed by the request. Ramon continued, "For those of you that don't remember our good friend Buddy Rosen — back with us again after living in Baltimore (whispering to Buddy) 5 years ago — Buddy's current address and phone number will appear in next month's issue of SOB Stories. Let's make Buddy feel welcome."

"Thank you Buddy. I try hard."

Buddy shook his head.

"So ... spill it." Kevin continued. "Got the call and you gave me some bullshit story about your parents being alive and Andi and Chrissy and you checking the flea market for aliens or something ... and ..."

"Kevin ... it's not a bullshit story. It's real."

"What's real ... the aliens?"

"No ... the part about my parents. They really might be alive."

"So let's go look for them. I'm game."

"Well ... it's not so easy. I'm not sure where to look. But I keep finding clues." Buddy reaches into his briefcase. He opened the notebook that he had just retrieved from the bank. "Check this out ... random ledger sheets, pictures, news clips ... "

"Hey ... can I keep this picture of the chick in the bathing suit?"

"That's my mother, putz." Buddy scoops up the notebook and puts it back in the briefcase. He pulls out one more document. "I found this sitting at the bottom of the safety deposit box ... all folded up." Buddy spread it out on the bar.

"It looks like a will."

"Yeah ... it's Abe's will ... and listen to this part: To my wife, Frances Rosen, I leave my entire estate including the Palms Motel ... and upon the death of my wife Frances, the remainder of this estate transfers to my son, Karl 'Buddy' Rosen ... and upon the death of Karl 'Buddy' Rosen, the remainder of this estate transfers to Save the Beaches Foundation, Inc." Buddy looks at Kevin. "What do you think about that?"

"Your real name is Karl?"

"Kevin ... will you focus!" He hits him on the side of the head. "This never made it to the courts. His whole estate went to Save the Beaches Foundation. I never saw a penny."

"That sucks." Kevin picks up the will to study the wording.

"I'm back." Debbie poured Buddy another beer even though his first was only half empty. "Hey Kevin, honey. Want your usual? Shirley Temple with an umbrella."

"Funny, Debbie ... you know I always use two umbrellas."

Debbie turns to the other bar patrons and yells, "You hear that, you derelicts? Two umbrellas. You can learn something from these guys ..."

Buddy put his head down and whispered. "Don't include me in the umbrella stuff."

"Is Manny here tonight ?" Kevin asked.

"Oh yeah, so is Cowgirl Candy." Debbie pointed to the end of the bar. Stacey was cornering Manny against the wall. She had her cowboy hat pulled over her braided long dark hair, tight black jeans, a fringed white shirt and boots. Candy was a regular at Manny's. Tonight she was holding a trophy that she won at the horse show in Tampa. She seemed to win as many trophies for horses as Manny and Debbie won for fishing. She was gushing all over Manny loudly telling him how wonderful he was. Debbie was not happy. "You know what I'd like to do with that trophy?"

"I'll do it for you, Deb," Jake the plumber, who was sitting next to Buddy, butted in.

"Jake, you're my hero. But you're so drunk, you wouldn't know how to find Candy's butt much less the trophy." Debbie emptied Jake's ashtray behind the bar and handed Buddy another beer almost in the same practiced move. "Thanks for the thought."

Through the front door came a skinny, disheveled, bearded blond-haired bum on a bicycle. His pants were torn at the bottom and came halfway up his thighs. His suit jacket was the same color, dirty beige and well worn. He threw the bike down in the middle of the floor. "Where's Manny? "

"Here, Billy." He started to walk toward him.

"How did we do?" Billy asked.

"I was just counting tonight's receipts. It was a good night." Manny answered. "Hey, Billy how about picking up the bike?"

"Oh, sure," Billy staggered around and picked up the bike. He added as he started out the door. "Keep up the good work."

Manny laughed and turned to see Buddy and Kevin. "Hey boys." He walked over to Buddy and threw an arm around him. "You don't look so hot."

"I bet you say that to all us derelicts, Manny." Buddy said as he looked at Debbie and winked at her. "And speaking of us derelicts, who the hell was that?"

"Billy? I guess you've never been here when he was." Manny said.

"He's a regular?"

"Oh yeah. Billy thinks he owns the bar... literally. He comes in once in a while to check on the receipts to see how his money's doing. Then he leaves a happy man." Manny said as he jumped behind the bar. "You know, Buddy, he's a young guy, only 28; he just looks older. His name's Billy Moore. Billy was a baseball star at Northeast High and was on his way to becoming a pro. Billy's dad lost his job and committed suicide.

Billy found him. He just flipped." He moved behind Deb and started to reach around her waist.

Deb moved away and elbowed him in the ribs. "Tired of horses are we?"

Buddy drained his glass and stood up, "Kevin. All this love and affection is just too much for me. I'll see you tomorrow."

"You leaving?" Kevin asked.

"Yeah ... gonna do some more ... reading." Buddy said.

Buddy slapped Kevin on the back as he chugged his beer causing him to spit all over himself. "Oops — sorry."

He leaned over the bar, high-fived Manny and kissed Deb.

The rains had come full force as Buddy stepped outside. He turned up his collar and headed to his car. Billy whizzed by and almost knocked Buddy over as he unlocked his door. He smiled as he looked at Billy turn the corner and disappear. "Good night, Billy." Buddy said aloud. "I hope the nightmares stop for you, too."

As Buddy grabbed the door handle, the windshield of his car exploded from the impact of a bullet fired from behind him. He turned in time to see a shadowed figure under an umbrella and a flash of light from a gun barrel. The second explosion paralyzed him with a searing pain in his chest.

As he fell to the street he thought he heard a voice say, "Sweet dreams, Buddy Boy."

FLASHBACK:

Frances and Abe Disappear

Buddy Rosen and Max Campbell loved to race down the beach on their bikes...playing cards clipped to the spokes, baseball caps backward on their flattops, bats slung on the side with saddle bags. Yes, they were the coolest racers on earth.

They had checkpoints. The Esso Station stop was first. Two root beers and two bags of sweet tarts would hold them over for a half hour until they reached the A & P. There they met Petey Mc Cabe, part-time bag boy and full time pal, in the parking lot for a cigarette. Petey seemed to always have access to single cigs. Sometimes Buddy stole a couple from Abe when he got too drunk to tell, but he was always afraid he'd get caught. Abe could get pretty nasty.

Saturdays were usually pickup game days. And when they didn't have enough players, they would have batting practice. Baseball was the only game. There was no other. The basketball courts got a workout from the high school kids, but none of the 10 year old beachers would even consider it.

This Saturday, it was just Max and Buddy. Petey was out of town with his family, the Haskell twins both had chicken pox, Billy Murphy and Patrick Callahan were cleaning up old man Shindler's garage for extra spending money, Fatty Hooperman went to the zoo with his sister and Sticks Sticklehauser, the skinniest kid in the third grade, had a leg cast that looked more like a sock on a toothpick.

"Max, the first one to the point gets the beer," Buddy yelled and pointed to the rock jetty that everybody called the point as they rode side by side on the beach road.

"And the sweet tarts?" asked Max.

"Ha, ha, you'll never learn, Red Baron." Buddy pedaled past Max.

"Cheater!"

"Oh I'll let you catch up, crybaby."

They both stopped to even up. Buddy counted down, "On your marks, get set..."

"Go."

The wind blew through their ears as the spokes clicked loudly with each rotation until they were just blurs. A hundred miles an hour...maybe 150...nobody could catch them. "Faster," Buddy thought. "I've got to get some extra speed ." He tried to put on an extra burst of speed but couldn't beat Max as he saw the point come closer.

Max skidded to a stop and dropped his bike as he leapt in the air shouting, "All right! Campbell leaves Rosen in the dust and the crowd goes wild."

Buddy couldn't stand to lose. "Jerk. I can beat you any time."

"Don't be a sore loser, Buddy."

"Forget it." Buddy spun his bike toward Franklin Field leaving Max behind to catch up. His heart was racing. Competition was so much a part of his makeup. When he was on the pitcher's mound, the anger would mount as he faced the batters. Abe called it his edge, " All great athletes feel that disdain for their opposition."

By the time they reached the field, Buddy's anger was gone. Max understood Buddy. They had been friends ever since Max had moved to John's Pass over three years ago. He knew Buddy's tantrums and how Buddy's dad acted when he drank. Max had seen him in action.

"You wanna catch?" Buddy asked as he took the mound.

"Sure Koufax. Burn it in there."

The afternoon showers hit hard just like they always did in August.

The sign on The Palms danced back and forth as the winds picked up on the Gulf. Frances closed the windows in the kitchen as she finished preparing the dinner meal for the 50 guests. Abe reached in his desk drawer to sip from the fifth of bourbon he kept for special occasions or, for that matter, any occasion.

"Ralph, take these bowls to Bernice and Selma."Frances said as she choreographed the table bussing. "Ask them to start with table 10 tonight. Audrey can have a plate of chicken if she'd like. Oh... and ask Buddy to come in to start the dishes."

"Ms. Rosen, Buddy ain't back from baseball yet."

"Did he call?" asked Frances.

"Don't know, ma'am. I'll ask Ms. Selma when I give her the trays."

Sounds of dishes and silverware clinking filled the air of Coconuts, The Palms dining room, as more guests started to arrive. John Cabrera sat with his wife Sally and their three-year-old daughter Mary. They had driven from New Orleans two days before. His law firm represented a builder in Tampa so John combined business with pleasure. They were the first to be seated. John was still feeling felt a little guilty about not eating breakfast at the hotel. Sally wasn't. In fact she had just argued about dinner before they came downstairs. "John, you act like they're paying us," Sally had told him. "Frankly, I don't like the food here and I want to eat at the seafood restaurant next door." John promised to go there tomorrow.

The Olsen clan came next. They took up three tables. Grandma Margaret and Grandpa Albert Olsen were celebrating their 50th anniversary and their whole clan came. Two sons, a daughter, a daughter-in-law, a son-in-law, and five grandchildren. They were from Eau Claire, Wisconsin and all lived within 10 square blocks of each other. All, that is, except for Andy Olsen, who went to Michigan State and would probably go into the hardware business with the rest of his family after he graduated.

The lights flickered in Coconuts as the lightning flickered outside.

"Lightning capital of the world, you know," Jayne Brandt told George Adams at her table. George was a 48 year old confirmed bachelor who looked and acted like he was 68. He owned a small accounting firm in Cincinnati. Jayne and her three beautiful daughters were from St. Petersburg. Recently divorced, Jayne decided to spend a weekend on the beach with her kids while they were still teenagers.

"I understand that this area also has the highest electrocution fatality rate in the country." George stated.

"Only if you count the death row prisoners," Jayne nudged George as her daughters chuckled. George sat without expression.

Jayne didn't give up. "It's a joke, George." He smiled politely.

Selma and Bernice busily served the bowls of fried chicken, mashed potatoes, green beans and rolls while taking drink orders. "And for you lovebirds. Would you like some tea or a soda? "Selma asked honeymooners Tony and Sylvia Diaz, who were cuddled in the corner table holding hands. Married for exactly 26 hours 18 minutes and 23 seconds, the Diazes flew in from Jersey and this was their first appearance since they got there.

Tony said, "Tea for both of us. Four lemons, right, Syl?"

"And a Sweet and Low, honey," Sylvia whispered.

"Need anything else," Selma said.

"Nothing," they said at the same time.

"I can see that." Selma smiled at them and turned to Kay Beytin's table.

Kay was a nurse from Akron, Ohio and sat with the gay couple Troy Martin and Blaise Graham, two local artists who lived on Bay Road, close to the hotel. They were frequent diners and big fans of Frances's home cooking.

Absent, as usual, were the Katz sisters, who usually ate from a hot plate in their room. Rarely did they leave. No one ever saw them on the beach or even out for a walk. When they left, they would bundle up in heavy clothing with scarves and sunglasses. Some said that they were once Hollywood starlets. Abe laughed at the suggestions. "Hollywood starlets, huh," he said to Frances one day. "Maybe they costarred with Lon Chaney or Bela Lugosi. You know, now that I think about it I did notice Isabel's chin yesterday. It was covered with werewolf fur."

The front door flew open just as there was a colossal thunderclap.

All eyes were on Buddy, who stood soaking wet at the opened doorway. It was as if everything was frozen in time without sound or movement. If someone were to take a picture of the Olsen family at that instant it would show a sea of opened mouths. George Adams had literally spilled his tea all over himself and Jayne Brandt.

The silence was broken by Audrey, who brought Buddy a towel and closed the door. Frances had come out of the kitchen at the same time.

"Buddy. My God, boy. Look at you." Frances started to dry his hair and saw that his scalp was bleeding. His shirt was torn off his right shoulder and he was covered with mud. "Are you all right ?"

"Mom, it's Max he's...he's...." Buddy couldn't finish.

"What Buddy? What about Max ?"

"He ...we ... well, we raced home ...I was in the lead... you know we had a fight before and well ... I was a jerk..."

"Buddy, what happened to Max?"

"A car ... I couldn't see it...I guess it skidded in the rain ...and it ... it ... hit him. God, Mom, I wish I would have never gotten mad at him...I think he was letting me beat him." Buddy burst into tears and Frances held him tight.

"Buddy, Buddy, it's not your fault. It's not your fault."

"Well look who's finally here...Mr. Hot Shot Baseball Player..." Abe staggered into the Dining Room.

"Abie don't ..." Frances tried to quiet him.

"Hanging on to Mommy's apron strings, I see...Well what you gotta say for yourself ?"

Frances stepped in front of him. “Abie, you don’t know what you’re saying.” The guests were now in total shock. It was a mixture of horror and embarrassment. Abe pushed Frances against the wall. “Hey, son. I’m talking to you. You missed your chores. Guess who had to cover for you. “

“I couldn’t help it dad....”

In mid-sentence Abe shot a slap across Buddy’s face that landed him in a heap on top of his mother. “There’s a little help for you. And here’s a little more.”

Abe stood over Buddy, ready to slap him again when a hand grabbed his wrist on the way down. He looked squarely in the face of Ralph Jennings.

“No, Mr. Rosen. Don’t hit the boy no more.” Ralph held his wrist tightly as he spoke.

Abe stood there with Ralph in an awkward dance pose, arms in the air, face to face. Suddenly the realization of where he was and who was watching hit him. He looked at the guests and then at his family crumpled against the wall. He wrenched his hand out of Ralph’s grip with a swift pull. “Hell with you. Hell with all of you.” He stumbled out of the dining room back into his office.

Ralph helped Frances to a chair and Selma took Buddy to his room to clean him up.

“Are you okay, Ms. Rosen?” Ralph asked.

“Yes, Thank you, Ralph.”

“You know, Ms. Rosen, Mr. Abe don’t really know what he’s doin’ when he’s like that. I remember when I was drinking. Sometimes, it was days before I even remembered what I did.”

“You are a good friend to Abe, Ralph,” Frances looked at the door to the office. “Maybe his only friend.”

Frances noticed Audrey peeking around under Ralph's arm. In one hand, she held her doll by the hair and the other hand grasped Ralph's tool belt. Frances moved close to her face, and Audrey hid her head behind Ralph. "Audrey, thank you, too. You were the only one with enough sense to help Buddy when he came in."

Ralph nodded his head and looked down at Audrey. "Ms. Rosen's talkin' to you, Aud. Quit buryin' your head."

Audrey buried her head further. Frances said, "That's okay, darling. You don't have to if you don't want to. I was just as shy at your age."

"Excuse me, Ms. Rosen."

Frances looked up. "Yes Bernice. What is it?"

"Officer Quinlan's here to see you."

Bernice stepped aside and Michael Quinlan raised his hand in a half wave. "Hi Frances. Sorry to bother you."

Frances led him into Buddy's room.

"He just fell asleep, "Selma whispered as they walked into the room.

"I don't want you to wake him," Quinlan began, "I guess he's been through a pretty rough experience. I can talk to him when he's feeling better."

"Would you like some coffee?" Selma asked.

"If it's already made. That would be just fine, thanks ma'am." Quinlan replied.

They walked out of Buddy's room and headed for the kitchen. Frances suddenly turned to Quinlan on the stairway, "Is Max...?"

"...in critical condition at the hospital. It doesn't look too good I'm afraid."

Frances shook her head and led them into the kitchen. Selma was already there pouring the coffee.

Quinlan continued as they sat at the counter. "The driver got away. There were reports of a gray pickup truck swerving down Bay Road, close to the accident. But, from the way the accident site looked, I think Max might have spun out of control and landed under the vehicle. The bike was in the middle of the street."

"Oh, my God." Selma said. "Buddy would be devastated if he knew that. He's already racked with guilt about this."

"Why is that, Selma?" Frances asked.

"He said that he and Max were fighting about winning some race or something. Buddy felt Max was trying to let him win." Selma brought a cup of coffee to Quinlan. "Do you take cream or sugar?"

"No this is fine, thanks. Did Buddy say anything else?"

Selma thought for a second. "Just that he didn't see much of what happened from where he was."

Michael turned to Frances, "Does he need to go to the hospital tonight? "

"I think he's okay." Frances said. "Just shaken up. What do you think, Selma?"

"Well, I washed his head with a wet cloth and there were some little cuts that caused a lot of blood. I think he just need to rest."

"Selma, you are a saint." Frances hugged her sister-in-law.

"Oy, I hope not."

"Well, saints or not, you two should get some sleep yourselves." Quinlan headed for the door. "Oh, I almost forgot. Is Abe still up?" Quinlan asked.

"Um ... I'm sure he's sleeping. Is there anything I can tell him for you?"

"I thought he might like to know that Mrs. Katz made another complaint this afternoon. "

"She did? Was it about Ralph?"

"It was ... how did you know?"

"Just a guess. She is always ... so ... cruel to him. Should I get Abe?"

"We'll go over it tomorrow, get some sleep. Thanks for the coffee."

As he headed toward his car, Michael Quinlan made a quick notation in his notebook .

Abe was snoring loudly.

Frances quietly undressed and went to the bathroom to wash her face. She looked into the mirror and felt her heart literally skip a beat. Her chest began to have that tightening that she felt on and off for the past four months. Numbness crept into her fingertips. That awful hopelessness fell over her. It always followed. The feeling that she was going to die. This has got to change.

There in the bathroom, listening to Abe snoring, Frances decided.

She finished washing and brushing. She slipped into bed next to Abe and she opened her diary. Her entry tonight would be a turning point. A new direction. The tightness subsided the more she wrote. The numbness disappeared. No more death. Only renewed hope and a chance at a new life.

"There. I've put it on paper. I'm not afraid of it. It makes perfect sense," she thought to herself. Then she did something that she rarely did since she started her diaries. She pulled out older diaries and flipped back through the pages to read entries.

"Why haven't I done this more often?" she thought. "Isn't that the purpose of keeping a diary after all?"

... January 10, 1948

My first entry in my journal as a New Yorker! Doesn't it sound wonderful...a New Yorker! No more little Frannie Eliot from Hicksville Alabama. Now I am Frances Eliot of New York City, thank you very much...

Frances chuckled aloud as she read. "When was I this young and naive?"

...I already met a friend on the first day. His name is Abe Rosen. I guess he's a Jew. My first friend ... and my first Jew...

Now Frances burst into laughter. Abe rolled over. "That you Frannie? What's so funny?"

"Nothing Abie. Go back to sleep."...You little Jew, you. Frannie laughed to herself now. How could she ever have said that in her diary?

...He's very handsome. He gave me a ride in his taxi and didn't even charge me. Mother was wrong. New Yorkers aren't mean and selfish. Everyone has been generous and kind.

Frances flipped ahead.

... April 23, 1948

Abie asked me to marry him. I'm so confused. He's so wonderful. He's already taught me so many things about life. What should I do? I feel there are so many things I want to do and experience. But I love Abie. I want to be with him. I guess I'll say yes.

"I guess I'll say yes?" Frances thought. "That's how I made one of the most important decisions in my life?" The tightness came back into her chest. Again she went ahead.

... December 25 , 1948

I miss not celebrating Christmas. Abie says it's just another way that retailers can make a buck. He doesn't care about any holidays. Even his own.

His drinking has gotten a little excessive. He won't agree, but I see a change in him I don't like. I know money's a little scarce and Abie has had bad luck lately at the racetrack. He doesn't bet too much and I hate to spoil his one pleasure, but I'm really worried about our future...

"Hate to spoil his one pleasure. What was I, chopped liver?" Frances started to question herself as she lay in bed next to the "man of her dreams".

... February 15, 1949

Mr. Simmons called again. He wants an answer about the modeling job. Abie doesn't want me to be gone for a week. I keep telling him that the pay would be more than I could make all year as a hostess at the Oasis. He's a little jealous, I think. Mr. Simmons has called a lot lately.

Last night Abie got a little too rough. We argued about his gambling and he pushed me against the dresser. He apologized over and over this morning. He's like a bad little boy when he's apologizing. It's hard to stay mad at him.

Frances' eyes welled up with tears.

... June 2, 1949

Abie's a hero!

He saved a passenger's life. The Times did an article about it. He gave this guy artificial respiration and got him to the hospital in time. He's some kind of big shot from Florida. Owns lots of land there. I'M SO PROUD OF HIM. He's been telling all his friends at Frankie's Bar about it. They stay all night talking about it...

"Good old Mr. J.D. Bowland..."

... December 1, 1949

Well it looks like we really are going to Florida.

Mr. Bowland's been after Abie to manage his motel in St. Petersburg. Abie doesn't know the first thing about managing a motel, but he says we can learn. I have to admit that it's a heck of a lot better than what we've got now. I don't know though. I don't like that Mr. Bowland. He gives me the willies. Every time he visits he grabs me in the rear and whispers obscenities. I haven't told Abie. He thinks Mr. Bowland is the Messiah. Maybe things will get better in Florida.

I'll tell him about the baby tomorrow……

Frances put down the book and began to drift off to sleep. "Enough history for one night," she thought. "Tomorrow starts a new chapter in my life."

Senator James Bennett and his entourage arrived at exactly 2:00 PM.

Phillips took the lead as usual. He was the power behind the throne. Phillips looked like a Chihuahua sniffing the road ahead for any signs of trouble. Small and thin, his frame could barely support his 5-foot-3 inch, 135-pound carriage. When he was younger, Phillips ate three milk shakes a day to try to fatten himself up. He hated being small. "Mr. Rosen, good to see you again." He greeted Abe with outstretched hand and his ever formal manner.

"Mr. Phillips, welcome back to the Palms." Abe shook his hand warmly and then reached around him to greet the Senator. "And let me say what a pleasure it is to welcome you both, as well."

"Well my friend, you have always been a most generous innkeeper. Your accommodations are superb. I don't think I gave you a VIP card to my restaurant, Capitol Club, for you and your family, did I?" The Senator asked.

"Why I don't think so, Jimmy. Thank you very much." Abe smiled to himself thinking about the three other cards in the top drawer of his desk from prior visits.

Frances walked up to Abe as he was shaking hands.

"Hello, Frances," said Bennett. "I've been thinking about your phenomenal cooking." He had practically fallen over himself when got to the word feenominal.

Mrs. Bennett chimed in, "Frances, you must give me your delicious recipe for that tender fried chicken of yours. Jimmy loves it so. He just can't get enough of it. "

That's not the only tender chicken he can't get enough of, Frances thought to herself.

"Why it would be an honor."

Bennett took his wife's hand and led her over to Abe and Frances. He stepped between them and placed an arm around Frances. "Let's get a picture. Phillips, would you do the honors? "

Phillips brought out the camera from his canvas bag. He made some minor adjustments (while Bennett did a few adjustments on Frances' waist), focused and said, "Say graft and corruption!"

"Cheese!" Senator Bennett said.

Abe called Ralph over and handed him two keys. "Ralph please take the Senator's luggage to Room 11 and Mr. Phillips to Room 26."

"Yessir." Ralph piled up the luggage on an old hand truck.

"Ralph will take care of you. Just in case you don't remember, meal times are noted here," Abe pointed out the section in the brochure that he handed to Phillips. "If there is anything else you need, please let us know."

"We thank you, Mr. Rosen." Phillips shook hands again. "And Mrs. Rosen," Phillips rescued Frances from Bennett's grasp, "We look forward to seeing you at dinner."

"Yes, we certainly do." Bennett said, as he extended his hand. Frances smiled and shook hands all around.

Senator Bennett didn't have the regal silver haired look of a senior politician. He was more the overweight, balding, "good ol' boy" type of politician that everyone in his home county of Sumter could relate to. He spent most of his adult working life in state politics: Councilman, School Board Commissioner, County Commissioner, and finally, State Senator.

At 65 years old, James Bennett was now one of the most powerful men in the state of Florida. He considered himself a man of the people ... protecting their land from anyone and everyone who would harm it. Being a man of the people was not easy. "The people" were constantly changing (depending on what side of the protection they were on). Sometimes he was a man of the developers ... sometimes he was a man of the environmentally friendly ... sometimes he was a man of the beach bums ... but he was always a Son of a Beach.

Actually, he was THE original Son of a Beach. He also founded the Save Our Beaches Foundation when there was very little commercial development on the beaches ... only small motels like The Palms. He was passionate about the beach. He had been ever since he spent the first night at the Palms more than 10 years ago.

It was also the day he met Oscar Martinez.

Oscar was a Cuban immigrant who made his living as a fisherman ... one of many ... living in the little beach community named Pass-a-Grille. Oscar had moved there with his young family. Fisherman gave Pass-a-Grille its name ... derived from the cooked fish on the beaches in grills seen by boaters as they motored through the pass.

The Bennetts had wandered into a little restaurant just a few steps from The Palms. The aroma of the fish grilling on open fires was intoxicating to Jim and Beverly. The restaurant was small but airy with wooden picnic tables set up outside on the beach.

Maritsa Martinez greeted the Bennetts. "Welcome to La Parrilla. My name is Maritza and I will be taking care of you tonight."

"Fantastic. Mmmmmm ... food smells great," James noted. "Okay to take a table outside?"

"Certainly."

The restaurant was a family affair. Maritza and her sister in law Rosalyn were waitresses, Oscar and his brother Juan were the cooks and even Oscar's young son Ramon bussed tables.

The food was incredible ... fresh snapper surrounded by fresh grilled vegetables, Cuban bread and sangria.

"Maritza," Bennett called out, "I must compliment the chef."

"Sure, sure ... I will get him," Maritza said. A few minutes later, Oscar Martinez appeared and exchanged pleasantries with Bennett.

"We are honored to have you visit us, Senator Bennett ... and Mrs. Senator Bennett." Oscar stammered.

"It's Jim and Bev," Bennett smiled at the last reference to Mrs. Senator Bennett. "You catch your own seafood, Oscar?"

"Yes ... yes. My brother and I are partners in the fishing boat and this restaurant. We both came over from Cuba together."

"You seem to be thriving here."

"Well, we are making a living and love being here." Oscar shook his head, breathed a heavy sigh and looked to the horizon.

"Is there something wrong, Mr. Martinez?" Beverly asked.

“Oh, pardon me ... I was just looking at the dredging equipment that was just put up last week.”

“Dredging?” Bennett asked. “What are they dredging here?”

“Well ... the Caprisi Company contracted with McCabe Marine to dredge the beaches from south of us to north of Clearwater over the next 10 years.” Oscar said. “You see ... through erosion ... the beaches are getting narrower and dredging will widen them again.”

“Yes ... Caprisi ... I know the CEO of that company. Good man ... good man.”

“Senator. I don’t think that he understands the harm he may do to the beach community. I know it provides more land in which he might develop more real estate but there’s a danger.”

“I thought you said it was good for the beaches.”

“Well ... it is ... it may save the beaches. But it also kills the natural environment at the same time. Sea turtles will be destroyed as will their nests. Silt and debris will be overturned and destroy other marine animals. Fishing will never be the same.”

“I see.” Bennett was deep in thought. ”Interesting. This is a real boom time for real estate, Oscar. I hear from developers and builders every day.”

“There may be no Florida left if they are not careful.”

That night, with Oscar Martinez’s help, James Bennett started looking at ways to protect the beaches by putting in dredging safeguards and formulated a plan to develop the Save Our Beaches Foundation. Bennett was making his own not-so-philanthropic mental notes as well... as politicians often do.

Developers were supportive of the safeguard measures (they had to be or they would not get state approval for their projects). The Foundation brought in support not only from Developers but from individuals as well.

The Sons Of the Beaches was born.

These were the locals, the visitors and the businessmen (yes … men only at that time) who contributed to the cause and helped to create a large endowment for the Save Our Beaches Foundation to continue their work. There had been only two Presidents of the Foundation: Bennett followed by Martinez.

Abe Rosen was an early member. It was a good thing for him to do politically and made sense to him from a business perspective. He was never an environmentalist … he left that to Frannie.

"Abe, I must talk to you." Frances said as the Senator's party moved out of earshot.

"Okay, I know I acted badly last night. I'm sorry. I got a little looped. It won't happen again."

"I know it won't, Abie. That's what we need to discuss," Frances was calmer than she thought she'd be. The words were really a relief to say. She had made her decision and it was the best she had felt in years.

Abe didn't catch the true meaning in her response. "Selma told me everything this morning. Is Buddy okay?"

"He went back to sleep. The doctor came over and gave him something to settle him down. He was still upset about Max."

"And about me too, probably."

"You didn't help matters any." Frances took a deep breath. "Abe ... we need some alone time. There are a few things I need to talk to you about."

"I've got an idea. How about taking the boat out tomorrow." Abe said as he came around the desk to give Frances a hug.

Frances held out her hand to stop him. "And what about the motel? Did you forget we have a motel to run? Just what do you plan to do about that minor problem?"

"We'll only be gone for a few hours. Selma, Ralph and Bernice can handle it."

"The last time you said that, there was a fire in the kitchen."

"Yeah, but this time we have insurance."

"Funny," Frances countered. "Well ... okay. Sure let's get away tomorrow."

"Great. Now back to work. Into the kitchen with you." Abe said in a mock dictatorial voice. "I have to pay the bills."

"How do you always get the job that only takes five minutes?"

"Five minutes? Are you kidding? We have tons of bills."

"But we have no money."

"True."

Buddy woke up groggy. He headed out into the hallway, and couldn't quite get his eyes opened. He thought he walked into the kitchen but he was wrong. He was still on the second floor.

"What are you doing in here?" Isabel Katz screamed and grabbed Buddy by the ear.

The sound and the pain were excruciating. Buddy couldn't break free. "You nasty boy. You should be ashamed. What are you doing here, I said?"

"I made a mistake, Ms Katz. Please let go of my ear."

"You and your drunken father and your goyisha mother. Your family are all after me. Did your father send you in to spy on me ? Is that why you're here?" The pain now radiated all the way to Buddy's toes. His anger mounted. The groggy feeling turned to an adrenalin rush that gave him renewed strength to deal with this onslaught. "Yes, that's it isn't it? Wasn't it enough that I dropped the complaint with the police after he called my sister to threaten her? I should call the police to tell them about you ...you ... horrible little boy..."

"I don't know what you're even talkin' about you crazy old fart." Buddy pulled loose finally and started to feel his ear again.

"Oh! Oh! Oh! See what I mean. You are your father's son. Just like him. Mmmph! How insolent!"

"I hope you and that other crazy sister of yours get hit by a bulldozer or something." Buddy was now squarely in front of Isabel Katz, fists clenched tightly.

"Get out. Get out this minute before I call the police. I swear I'll call them." Isabel wagged the only ringless finger on her chubby hand in Buddy's face. The fat on her arm swung back and forth as the bracelets on her wrists clinked up and down.

Buddy turned sharply and smashed his fist into the wall causing one of the pictures to crash to the floor. "Good! Good!" Isabel screamed. "That belongs to the gonif, your father. Let him deal with you."

He slammed the door behind him, tears streaming down his face.

In the kitchen, Bernice was singing the last strains of Just A Closer Walk With Thee as she cleaned the last of the mornings dishes. The smell of coffee still hung in the air. Outside the window, Bernice could see Audrey Jennings playing tea party with her baby doll.

"Bernice, got any more of that coffee left?" Albert Olsen asked from the kitchen doorway. Bernice turned off the water and started to get it for him. "No need to wait on me. I'll just make myself at home if that's all right with you."

"Lawd yes, Mr. Olsen. The coffee pot is right over by the window. Cream is in the icebox and sugar next to the pot."

"Thanks, Bernice. I decided to take a walk this morning. Looks like I walked right through breakfast, didn't I ?"

"You still hungry? I could make you some eggs or maybe french toast."

"You are kind. But I just want coffee this morning." Olsen looked out the window at Audrey who now had additional guests at her tea party, two of the Olsen grandchildren.

"Bernice, is Ralph Jennings ...um ... okay?"

"How so, Mr. Olsen?"

Olsen thought a minute about how he asked the question. "I guess I mean is he just kind of slow or does he have other... problems ?"

"Oh, Ralph's a good man. He had a hard life, Mr. Olsen. Guess you heard he spent some time in prison."

"My wife told me he spent time for theft, or something."

"Yes, sir that's right. Theft. He had some bad times.

Audrey was just a baby and needed an operation to help her hear better. She had a bone in the way of her eardrum, I think. Ralph had just lost his job and his wife left him and took all the savings and everything else except for Audrey. Ralph got pretty desperate. He robbed a gas station with a squirt gun. Got 5 years. But with good behavior, he was out in a year."

"Has he been here long?"

"Been here for about two years ever since he was released. actually, Mrs. Rosen hired him to do some odd jobs and he just never left."

"And Audrey?"

"She had the operation two years ago. Still doesn't talk, but the doctors say she is able to. Just don't want to, I suppose. She's really a very smart girl ... just a little on the shy side, with people, you know what I mean? She's a tall girl, so you'd think she's older, too. Fools most people when they meet her." Bernice took out the mop and pail. She started to fill the bucket.

"Well, let me get out of your hair, Bernice, so you can get some work done. Thanks for the coffee."

"You're most welcome, Mr. Olsen. Tomorrow, why don't you try the whole meal?"

Abe heard the sobs through the bedroom door. He slowly opened the door and saw Buddy lying on his stomach crying in his pillow. He closed the door quietly and knocked on the outside. "Hey, Buddy, can your old stupid man come in?"

Buddy stopped but kept his face in the pillow. "Just a minute." He jumped up and splashed water on his face in the sink and wiped it off with a towel. He opened the door.

"Hey," Abe said.

"Hey," Buddy replied. He looked up at Abe for a few seconds.

"Can I come in?"

"Guess so." Buddy stepped aside to let him in.

"You okay?"

"Yeah."

"Mad at me?"

Buddy didn't answer. He looked out the window at the sunbathers on the beach.

"I know I screwed up. I heard about Max. I'm just glad you're okay. You know, I don't know what your mother and I would do if anything like that ever happened to you."

Abe put a hand on Buddy's shoulder. They looked at each other for a minute and then both hugged.

"Can we go see Max?"

"He's not able to have visitors right now. But we will go see him when he's up to it."

Buddy put his head down. Abe saw a little fresh blood on his neck. "Buddy are you bleeding ?" He reached over to wipe it and showed Buddy.

"It's my ear, dad."

"What happened to your ear."

"Mrs. Katz...she... pulled it."

"She what!" Abe saw red. His blood pressure climbed.

"I accidentally walked into her room. I was a little dizzy this morning. She got angry and said some pretty mean things to me. I guess I kinda did back at her too."

"Well I guess I'll have a few words with her myself."

"No dad. I don't care anymore. It's not important."

"It is to me," Abe steamed.

"Buddy, you're awake," Frances said as she stepped into the room. Next to her was Michael Quinlan. Abe quickly turned to face them both. "You look like you're feeling better."

"Uh, huh," Buddy nodded.

"Here you go, slugger." Quinlan handed Buddy the baseball mitt he lost the night before. "I guess you might be needing this soon."

"Oh, wow! You found it. Thanks." Buddy grabbed the mitt and hugged it to his chest.

"It was on the side of the road near the accident."

Abe extended a hand to Quinlan who shook it. "Thank you for bringing it back, Michael."

"Not a problem." He turned to Buddy. "Slugger, are you up to talking about the accident?"

"Um ... yeah, I guess so."

"What do you remember?"

"Well, me and Max had just left the field. It was getting late and the sky looked pretty bad."

"What time was that?" Quinlan asked as he took notes.

"I guess it was about 6 o'clock." Buddy looked over at his Dad sheepishly. He knew Abe would make a mental note of his lack of promptness. Abe raised an eyebrow, a sure sign that Buddy was right in his assumption.

"Just you and Max?"

"Yep."

"Go on."

"We headed down Bay Road when it started to rain. Hard. We raced each other home." Buddy swallowed hard and continued. "Max usually beats me. He's pretty fast. I think he was letting me win."

"Why did he let you win?"

"He beat me before we got to the field. I got mad at him. I was a ... you know ... sore loser."

"What happened next?"

"Well, I didn't see the accident. The only thing I saw was Max caught under the tires of the truck. He was screaming . I spun around and fell off the side of the road. I cut myself a little."

"Then you rode home?"

"Well I don't really remember. I got scared when I looked at Max and I was real close to home so I guess I just...." Buddy looked around at everyone.

"That's okay, Buddy." Quinlan tried to calm him. "People who are injured sometimes wander off without knowing where they're going. It's a kind of shock to their systems. Is there anything else you remember?"

"No. I guess that's all."

"If you do remember anything else tell your mom or dad to call me ... okay?" Quinlan asked.

"Sure."

"Thanks slugger," Quinlan said.

"I'll see you out," Frances replied as she walked him to the door. Once they were in the hallway she moved close to him and whispered,"Michael ... ?"

Abe yelled down the stairs, "Frannie, he wants a cold drink. Will you grab one from the kitchen?"

Frances paused, then called up to him. "I'll be right up."

Quinlan smiled. "The driver might have been reckless or Max might have accidentally slipped under his wheels. Either way, Buddy's not to blame."

"That's not what I was going to say, Michael." Frances handed him a folded note.

"I know." He closed the door behind him.

Mike stood on the porch for a few minutes. He thought about Frannie ... she was special. She had a great smile, a beautiful face ... even the first time he saw her. She had a bruise on her forehead and a few missing fingernails. "Silly me ..." she had said when he showed up at the motel after one of the guests called the police. "I lost my grip when I was carrying the laundry and took a terrible fall down the stairs."

He left his card and told her to call him day or night if there was any trouble.

She never did.

But he was drawn to her. At least twice a week, he found himself at Coconuts for lunch. Frannie sometimes sat with him and they talked about their lives ... their dreams. Frannie always had that look of vulnerability and a hint of pain that she just could not talk about.

The innocent lunches turned into not so innocent afternoons. Quinlan became an expert at creating stories at work and at home.

He read her note.

Now, it was time to make a decision.

Ann English put on her lipstick in slow careful motions. She sat in front of the vanity mirror admiring her features. "It's so easy to get what you want from men," she thought. Her looks were her ticket to fortune and she was determined to get more than her share.

She knew it long before she ran into Mr. I Can Make You Rich Phillips. The little weasel thought that if he'd introduce her to the rich and powerful she would in turn feel indebted enough to be his girl. Naturally, she did nothing to make him feel differently.

Before she remade herself, Ann English was Anna Jimenez. She worked as a legal secretary in the law offices of Stein, Blizzard, Campbell and Kroll. The firm was based in Tallahassee and represented many large developers and contractors in the state. Anna found herself involved in some of the lobbying efforts as an extension of her office duties. The partners noticed her attributes early and utilized her ability to open doors on a more frequent basis.

Anna met Phillips in a diner. During a break in the legislative session, they both wound up eating lunch in a diner next to the capitol building. She had noticed Phillips during the session. He couldn't keep his eyes off her. She walked into the diner and asked if she could sit at his table. The place was packed and seats were at a premium. He practically leaped to his feet. "Why certainly. Please. Have a seat."

"You work for Senator Bennett don't you?" Anna asked.

"Why yes. Yes I do." He could hardly contain himself.

"I'm Roger Phillips. And you are ..."

"Ann ... English." She read the first menu item "English muffins." Sounded like a good Anglo name to try out.

"... Anna Jimenez of Stein, Blizzard, Campbell and Kroll. Lobbyist for developers." Phillips caught her off guard.

"I'm so embarrassed."

"Hey. Don't be. It's the protected state land bill on the floor, isn't it? That's why you sat here. You want my help, don't you ?"

"Listen, I think I better just slink off to some other corner."

"Hey don't go. I can help you. You don't have to pretend in order to get to Senator Bennett. He listens to me. You can be Anna Jimenez or Ann English or Elvis Presley for that matter."

She got to Bennett all right. And she really got to Phillips. He was crazy in love with her. He took her everywhere and introduced her to everyone.

And here she was in the Palms Motel getting herself beautiful for Senator James T. Bennett. Phillips, her puppy dog, was standing guard out in the anteroom. Tonight, Jimmy Boy was going to bring her something expensive and ostentatious, her favorite two things. The phone rang twice. That was the signal. She slipped on her dress and put on her earrings. "Roger, do me, will ya?" She called through the open doorway.

"Anytime, gorgeous." Phillips reached around to zip her up. He paused and put his hands through her dress and around to her ample breasts.

"Down, boy. The master is arriving soon."

"That fat bastard. Sometimes I get crazy thinking about his pudgy, slimy claws all over your body."

"I keep telling you not to think about it so much. I don't think about it at all. It's just our means to an end. Besides this was your idea you know."

"I know, I know."

A knock on the door. Phillips looked through the peephole in the study and saw the top of the fatso's balding head. "Senator," he announced as he opened the door, "your chariot awaits."

Bennett walked past Phillips and stood in awe before the statuesque Ann English who sat at the corner of the bed with one long leg draped over the other. He turned to his trusty aide and as he closed the door said, "Keep a light on for me, Phillips."

"Yessir ... I'd like to put your lights out," Phillips quietly said as the door closed.

The night air was filled with a heavy, musky smell of salt water and sand.

Tony Diaz and his bride made a second rare public appearance. They embraced on a blanket at the edge of the water, barely noticing the ocean as it engulfed the sun on a canvas of reds and golds and deep blues.

The Olsen grandchildren were busy building a sand castle, which was almost demolished by Sally Cabrera when she started to accidentally step in the moat. John caught her at that crucial second.

On the porch sat the rest of the Olsen clan. "Mother, would you like to accompany me on a stroll by the water. Maybe you'll get lucky tonight." Albert said as he tickled Margaret in the ribs.

"You old fool," Margaret Olsen chided him while winking at her daughter, Ann Marie, "it's a wonder I even married him. I guess I'll have to walk with him to keep him quiet."

"If we're not back by midnight, don't look for us." Albert gave the okay sign to son Andy as Margaret nudged him in the ribs.

Oldest son, Al, Jr. had his nose buried in the newspaper. Doris, his wife of 7 years asked, "Al, You wanna take a walk, too?"

"Hmm?" Al continued to read.

"I asked if you wanted to take a walk with me."

"Mmm ..."

"Oh dear, the kids are drowning."

"What?!" Al jumped up and dropped the newspaper.

"Just kidding," Doris laughed. "I wanted to see what it would take to get you off your butt."

"Not funny, Do."

Al resumed his original position.

Inside, Frances, Bernice and Selma cleaned the kitchen while Ralph mopped the dining room floor. Audrey played hopscotch on an imaginary sidewalk in the front lobby. Abe poured over the bills in the office.

Buddy ran through the dining room and almost knocked over Ralph's bucket. "Hey, Buddy. Careful there, sport. The floor's wet you know."

"Sorry, Ralph." He turned and almost knocked over Audrey, too. She had come up behind him without a sound. Buddy practically tiptoed out the room.

Audrey walked over to one of the tables by the kitchen door. She crawled underneath and spotted something shiny. She picked it up and held it in her hand. Audrey looked over at Ralph who was bent over pushing the mop in long fluid strokes.

She put the pretty diamond and sapphire ring in her pocket.

"Esther, isn't Charlton Heston the most gorgeous thing you ever saw?" Isabel practically gushed as she and Esther walked out of the Center Theater. Not many things on this planet impressed Isabel Katz. Ben Hur was one of the chosen few.

"Personally, I like that handsome Kirk Douglas. He's a real mensch."

"And where is Ralph Jennings, that gonif?" Isabel crossed her short arms across her enormous bosom. "He was supposed to be here after the show. Probably holding up a jewelry store with the Rosen gang. Once a gonif, always a gonif I always say." She bobbed her head up and down.

"Now, Isabel, give the man a chance. He said he'd pick us up after he did the floors at the motel. He'll probably be here in a couple minutes."

Esther put an arm around Isabel.

"Floors, schmoors, he shouldn't keep two single ladies standing out here on the street. It's not safe." Isabel said.

"You want to wait inside?"

"And maybe miss him because he doesn't see us, no thank you."

Just as she answered, Ralph pulled up next to the curb. He jumped out and opened the rear passenger door. "I'm awful sorry about not being here when you got out. Have you been waiting long?"

"Hmph." grunted Isabel.

"No, Ralph. Not long at all." Esther added quickly.

Both climbed into the motel station wagon. "Well look Isabel. It's Ralph's little girl. Hi dear. Are you out for a ride with daddy?" Esther asked.

"Audrey don't speak ma'am." Ralph said as he got behind the wheel.

"Ever?"

"No ma'am."

"Probably one of those children who are just slow learners." Isabel added.

"I don't think so ma'am. The doctors say she did real good on all the written tests she took."

Isabel whispered to Esther just loud enough for Ralph to hear. "I'll just bet she got those retarded genes from her father."

"Isabel. You are horrible," Esther said.

"What's that ma'am?" Ralph asked.

"Nothing Ralph. We were talking about something else," Esther answered.

Audrey frowned as she looked out the window in the front seat and pulled at her dolly's hair. Then she remembered her new treasure. She reached in her pocket and took out the ring. Then Audrey combed the baby doll's hair into a ponytail.

She slipped the ponytail through the ring to hold it back. Looking at the new princess she had created made Audrey smile and hug her dolly.

"Well, here we are," Ralph announced as he pulled into the driveway of the motel.

"Oy, I would have never guessed," Isabel whined.

"Thank you, Ralph," Esther said as Ralph held her door open.

"You are very welcome. And my other special passenger ..." Ralph noticed that Audrey had fallen asleep. "Oh, my precious, let me carry you to the house."

Ralph picked her up and headed to the door behind the Katz sisters. He looked down at her angelic face and her smile as she clutched her. "Hello. What's this?" Ralph thought. He put Audrey down on a porch swing and took the ring from the baby doll's hair. "My God. This looks expensive. I wonder where Audrey got this." Ralph placed it in his pocket. "I'll give this to Mrs. Rosen tomorrow. Someone is probably looking for it."

The sisters stopped at the front desk to see if they got any messages. Seeing their box empty they scurried off to their room.

"Oh, Isabel. I wanted to show you what I discovered today." Esther clutched Isabel's arm.

"Tomorrow honey, tomorrow."

"Now don't be such an old woman. Come with me. You'll enjoy this."

Esther grabbed a flashlight from her room, took Isabel around the back of the motel and quietly came up to a place in the sand that looked like a mound with a hole behind it. She turned on the flashlight. "Shhh. Be careful, Isabel. Look."

"So what am I looking at?"

"This is a nest. A very special nest of turtle eggs. Sea turtles around here are known to build their nests in the sand. Isn't it interesting? There are hundreds of tiny eggs here.?

"Fascinating, Esther, now let's..."

Isabel was interrupted by the ring of a phone and a bright light that hit them both in the face through the adjacent window.

"Hello." James Bennett's voice bellowed through the open window. "Well... what is it?"

Esther scooted up to the window. "Isabel, it's the senator. Come here and look."

"Esther, you should be ashamed." Isabel tried to pull her arm away from the window, but Esther insisted on getting closer.

"He's got some woman with him. Oh my ... they both are naked as newborn babies, Isabel. She's scratching his back."

"I don't care what he tells you." Bennett continued, "That $25,000 was paid in full. You get Barody's name on the contract tonight ..."

Esther had her nose, appropriately enough, practically in the open window. She turned to Isabel. "Her head is under the covers. I wonder how he can keep his attention on the phone call."

"Good evening, ladies," said a voice from the shadows behind Isabel. It startled her so badly that she knocked Esther to the ground when she jumped back.

"Let me help you." He bent down to help her to her feet.

"Oh, how clumsy of me," Isabel said. "Thank you, sir. We were just over here, looking at sea turtle eggs."

Esther piped in, "Yeah, turtles. Obviously, I wanted a closer view at ground level."

"We haven't had the pleasure, have we?" Isabel extended her hand. "I am Isabel and this is my sister Esther. We are the Katz sisters."

"Nice to meet you. I am Roger Phillips, assistant to Senator James Bennett."

Isabel and Esther looked at each other. "Well," Esther said. "It's been a real pleasure, but my sister and I must be running now."

"Have a nice evening, ladies," Phillips said as they shuffled in the sand off to their rooms.

He glanced through the open window just as Senator Bennett turned off the light.

Frances couldn't believe it.

Abe was in the kitchen making sandwiches, filling the picnic basket with all kinds of goodies and singing. Yes, Abie was singing. She couldn't remember the last time, no, make that any time he sang.

"Abie, do you want me to call the doctor?" Frances touched his forehead.

"Surprised?" Abe asked.

"Shocked would be more like it."

"Well get used to it. This is the new Abe Rosen, family man, loving husband, caretaker extraordinaire, and whatever else there is. Today, my first official act as a human is to take you on an afternoon cruise. I've already hitched up the boat trailer."

"I am impressed."

"Me too."

"Lawd!" Bernice said as walked into the kitchen and put her purse in the closet.

"I see you know my formal name, Bernice," Abe replied.

"Ms. Rosen ... we in big trouble."

"I think you're right, Bernice. But until the sky falls let's enjoy it."

"You know there's just one thing I need a little help with, ladies," Abe said.

"Uh, oh," Bernice said. "Here it comes."

"Do I put wax paper on the sandwiches before the aluminum foil or ..."

"The sky just fell." Frances said and opened the drawer where the wax paper lived.

It was so hard to hate this man. How many chances had she given him? There were the late night calls from bookies and who knows who, asking for ... demanding repayment of gambling loans. Sometimes she was scared for her life and the lives of the whole family. Why couldn't he just have affairs like other husbands?

The calls still come. He didn't think she knew, but she did. The cars parked out front at different times of the day and night. His drinking had increased. He was afraid to go outside.

No, her plans hadn't changed. Nothing would dissuade her. But this morning was different.

Something felt strange.

Downstairs was a busy place at breakfast that morning. George Adams had planned a day of museum tours and during breakfast had actually asked Jayne Brandt to come along.

"Why George, or should I say By George..." Jayne said as she nudged him in the ribs, "I'd love to go with you."

George actually smiled and chuckled. "My mother used to say that to me all the time. By George, you're a smart one."

Jayne grabbed his hand and looked him squarely in the face. "George, please don't compare me to your mother. I know this sounds like a strange request, but I just got rid of a guy who did that to me all the time."

"Certainly, Jayne. I understand what you mean." Although George hadn't a clue. He loved his mother. He meant it strictly as a compliment.

The Olsens all were dressed in tee shirts that said "Olsens For 50 Years" with caricatures of Albert and Margaret. The picture was of Margaret standing over Albert with a rolling pin as he lay snoring in the bed.

The Cabreras tiptoed out, skipping breakfast once again. They were driving to Sarasota to shop and sightsee. Behind them were the Diazes, who had their beach blankets and a portable radio.

The Senator and his entourage walked briskly to two awaiting cars. Mrs. Bennett kept asking the same question, "But Jimmy, I don't understand why we have to leave so early. Is it so important that we head back right away?"

"Yes dear. I told you that I must get to Tallahassee as soon as possible. It's a matter that I can't discuss."

"Mrs. Bennett," Phillips picked up on the cues. "Please don't be mad at me. I am the one who gave the Senator the message about heading back to Tallahassee."

"Oh Mr. Phillips, I'm not mad. Just disappointed."

"I understand," Phillips said as he helped Mrs. Bennett into one of the cars. He turned to Bennett and continued, "Senator, I have some unfinished business here. I'll meet you in Tallahassee when I finish."

Bennett patted him on the back.

Selma scurried back to the kitchen for more coffee. "Abe, you get out of here. Bernice and I are in charge today. Hurry up now. Out with you."

Abe grabbed the picnic basket and turned to Frances. "Are you ready to go, gorgeous?"

"I am. But I better check on Buddy first."

Abe smiled (something he rarely did). "I talked to him before I came downstairs. He thought this was a great idea. He even helped me with the boat trailer."

"He did?"

"Sure he did. He made me promise me to take him out after I brought you back."

"Okay, enough talking. Go... Go... you two." Bernice and Selma almost said in unison.

"Come on, Frannie. This is called taking a little time for ourselves. We deserve it," Abe said as he gently pushed her out the door.

Buddy watched from his window as they pulled out of the driveway. When they were out of sight he ran out the back door and hopped on his bike, pedaling as fast as he could.

Esther awoke with a dull pain in her chest. She didn't want to tell Isabel, partly because she knew how Isabel fell apart in emergencies and partly because she didn't want to admit what she thought it was. She lay in bed for a little while longer, but it just got worse. Her left arm felt numb. She got scared. It was like that for 10 minutes and then subsided. She went back to sleep.

The alarm went off at 8:00.

"Esther, you awake?" Isabel picked up her head out of her pillow and hit the alarm button. "Esther?"

"Yes, Isabel I'm awake."

"So, let's get dressed. I want to get to the stores early to beat the crowds." Isabel headed to the bathroom to begin her morning ritual that Esther knew so well.

"You know, Isabel, I'm not up to shopping today."

"What, Esther? You not up to shopping? That's like saying the Pope's not up to being Catholic today."

"No, Isabel, you go ahead. I think I'll just catch up with some letter writing."

"Don't be ridiculous. You are going and that's that."

"I'm not going, Isabel."

Isabel came over to the side of the bed. She sat down next to her younger sister and asked: "You okay? "

"Yes, I'm okay." Esther was getting irritated.

"Well then, get your tush up and moving like a big girl."

"I am a big girl and I can think for myself. This morning I don't want to go shopping."

"Very well. If you're going to be that stubborn I guess I'll just have to cancel the shopping plans we had. Even though it was your idea to begin with. So what do you care if I can't get that purse. It's probably not going to be on sale for long and I'll miss it ..."

"Go get the purse. Go shopping already. Don't be such a kvetch about everything. Can't you do anything yourself. Do I have to be with you every second of the day?" Esther felt the chest pains coming back and bit her lip.

"Well, I never...." Isabel slapped her knees, stood up and headed back to the bathroom to finish her ritual. Esther's pain started to go away.

Ralph was washing the car.

Audrey had her bathing suit on and was filling the bucket, which of course meant that soapy water was overflowing out onto the driveway and the street. She loved helping him.

"Audrey, careful that you don't let out all the suds. Daddy won't have any left for the car."

Audrey looked in the bucket and picked up the hose. She forgot to check where she pointed. Water squirted all over Ralph. "Hey," he said and started to run around to the other side of the car. Audrey pointed the hose down and started to laugh.

Then she realized that she held the power to make him run. She followed him around the other side squirting him as she ran. He naturally played along until he sneaked behind her and tickled her. She turned quickly and she and Ralph pretended to wrestle. She aimed the hose. Ralph ducked. It hit Isabel right in the face as she stepped out on the porch.

Isabel screamed; then there was dead silence for a few seconds. "You horrendous creature. You should be locked up with the other retarded children and you...you...you sad excuse for a father...you shouldn't even be out of jail much less allowed to be around decent people."

Audrey started to cry. She dropped the hose and ran to the back of the house. Ralph was livid, "Ms. Katz, little Audrey and me was just playing. I'm sure sorry we got you wet. But that don't mean that you should call us those things."

"Is that so? Well just what would you call the type of people who shoot water at unsuspecting people? I will discuss this matter with your employer when I see him. Yes, I certainly will."

Isabel bustled down the stairs past Ralph and headed to the bus stop. Ralph used all his willpower to stop himself from tripping her, knocking her to the ground and beating the living hell out of her.

"Oh, Ms. Katz." Isabel and Ralph turned at the same time to face Roger Phillips.

"Oh hello, Mr. Phillips." Isabel said.

"I noticed you were heading to the bus stop. Can I give you a lift somewhere?

"Well that would be splendid. Are you going downtown, perhaps? I was going shopping today along Beach Drive."

"It just so happens that I am heading to an attorney's office just around the corner from the shops."

"Wonderful." She glowered at Ralph. "I guess there are still some gentlemen around after all."

Ralph watched them both walk to Phillips' car. Isabel looked back with that haughty look of hers and Ralph shot imaginary daggers at her eyes.

"Perfect," Frances yelled to Abe as he backed the trailer into the water. She traded places with him and got behind the wheel of the car. Abe jumped on the trailer and released the crank to float the boat into the water.

"Okay, Frannie, I've got her." Abe tied up the boat as Frances put the car in gear and pulled into a shady spot next to the dock.

The practiced moves of loading and unloading the boat trailer were now second nature to the Rosens. They used to practically live on their boat. Whenever they got the chance, they would take the boat out to fish, to ski or just to anchor and lay in the sun.

The semi-secluded spot they put in the boat had always been their "secret hideaway." Why so few people used it remained a mystery to Abe. There was an ideal turnaround and a natural slope to back onto. It isn't visible from the road and was probably used more often in the past by the old neighbors. The older beach homes were knocked down during the construction boom.

Abe watched Frances walk up to the dock. "You look as beautiful today as you did when we first met."

"Sure. I'm a regular vision with sweat dripping down my face and my hair must look just gorgeous."

"Yes it does."

"Okay Mr. New Man, let's shove off."

"I'm not finished my speech." The boat bobbed close to the dock as Abe put a foot out to protect it. Frances lowered the basket into one of the seats and stepped in the boat. "I love you Frannie." Abe looked at Frances with an expression that was a little removed and a little frightening to her. "I should have told you that many times and was just too stupid not to."

"I love you too Abie." Frances grabbed Abe around the neck and kissed him on the cheek. His expression remained motionless. "Can we leave now?"

"We've got time. We've got plenty of time. After all, we've got our whole lives ahead of us, don't we Frannie?"

"Abe, what are you talking about?"

"I'm talking about your diary, Frances. I read it last night and I know what your plans are."

"How dare you! How dare you read my diary."

"How dare me? You must be confused, dear."

"My diary is private." Now Frances was screaming at Abe through tears streaming down her face. She stood and held onto the boat rail for balance. "You have no right ..."

"No right? No right? I have every right." Abe reached out and grabbed Frances by the collar. "I am your husband, 'til death do us part."

"Abe, you're scaring me."

"You were going to leave me, Frannie, weren't you?" Abe put his other hand around Frannie's throat and started to squeeze. "I'm just having a streak of bad luck. You know that."

"Abie...I can't breathe ..."

"Maybe there's somebody else. Maybe you are having an affair with that sleaze from New York."

"You're ... crazy ... Abie ..." Frances began to lose consciousness. The blackness started to overtake her. Explosions erupted in her mind's eye.

"Yeah, maybe it's that guy who was going to make you a star. You always did want to be a star, didn't you ..."

Frances hung lifelessly in Abe's grasp. He still squeezed her throat, shaking her violently.

"No you're not going to leave me. You're never going to leave me ..."

Abe didn't see the rock as it came down on his head from the back with enough force to send him and Frances into the boat.

"That's for you, bastard."

Isabel looked out the window of the bus and felt cheated out of her whole day.

First she got the cold shoulder from Esther. That wasn't like her. She couldn't remember the last time Esther didn't want to go out. It was usually Isabel that had to be convinced. And Esther was so short with her.

Then Ralph's horrid child sprayed her. That Mr. Phillips had been kind enough to take her to the shops, but kept asking her so many questions. She couldn't seem to shake him. It got so late by the time she got started shopping that she couldn't get to all the stores she wanted to.

It was getting dark when Isabel finally reached the motel and the rain had stopped.

She passed Ralph, who looked up for a moment. He was emptying the trash next to the front desk. She headed straight to her room without recognizing his presence.

Isabel stopped to take out her room key and accidentally dropped her purse spilling the contents out all over the floor. Sighing, she bent down to pick up all her belongings when she realized that the strap on her old purse had ripped. Isabel cursed under her breath. She looked up to the heavens as if to say, “Why me?” and leaned against the door. She felt it give way.

"That’s funny,” Isabel thought as she pushed the door open further. “Esther wouldn’t leave this unlocked.”

As she stepped inside, Isabel tripped over something in the middle of the floor. “Oh my…,"Isabel turned on the light switch. “What the … ?”

It was a mixture of revulsion and anger that Isabel felt as she looked at what remained of her motel apartment. She had fallen over the living room table, which was lying on its side in the middle of the floor along with sofa cushions and magazines. Everywhere there was destruction. Drawers were pulled out and personal items were strewn out along the floor.

She was sickened by the fact that someone actually broke into their room, their private world and went through their personal belongings and was furious that they caused this kind of destruction. Where was Esther?

“Esther,” she yelled, “Esther …”

She looked in the bedroom and saw more of the same. The mattress was off the bed and pulled apart; the suitcases were thrown open; clothing strewn across the floor, night tables pulled over.

“Esther, are you here?”

Her jewelry box lay open in the corner empty. Isabel felt the familiar rush of anger come to her cheeks. She rushed to the closet and reached up to the top shelf. The movie camera was still there. She was in a trance as she looked through the viewfinder. "I'll show them. I'm not going to take this lying down. I need to keep a record of what they did. I know who it is. Those horrid Rosens. They did this. I hate them. They'll pay. They — " She stopped and dropped the camera.

"Oh my God. Esther."

Esther lay on the floor between the bed and the wall. Her eyes were still opened but her skin and her lips had the look of death. She was still wearing her nightgown.

Isabel leaned over and tried to pick her up, but Esther fell in a heap on the floor.

Suddenly, from behind her, Isabel felt a hand grab her hair and pulled back her head so hard that she dropped to her knees. Her neck felt the cutting of the cold, sharp blade and the wet gush of her own blood as it rushed from her neck.

By the time Detective Quinlan got to the crime scene, the motel was swarming with police, news cameras and gawkers. "Who found them?" Quinlan asked an officer on the scene as they stood over the bodies of Esther and Isabel Katz.

"The little girl, Audrey. She's the handyman's kid."

"Shoot it," Quinlan said to the police photographer who had just taken the rest of the room and was waiting for the okay from Quinlan.

"Anything in particular?"

"Yeah, make sure you get the walls and floors where the blood hit."

Quinlan felt that sick sensation in the pit of his stomach. He didn't know if it was from the blood-soaked sisters or because he felt responsible for dropping the ball when they dropped the complaint. The beach had its share of crazies and bar fights but homicides were not typically on the menu.

Also not typical was a visit by Chief Stevens, but there he was big as life swaggering up to Quinlan. "Mike," Stevens said as he pulled him aside. "I understand these sisters filed a complaint — with you."

"That's right, Chief. But they ..."

"... I know ... I know ... not unusual. Filed a complaint every year, right?"

"Right, although this one was a little different. She was missing some jewelry. There was one ring that Isabel Katz was particularly fond of ... but she couldn't be sure if she brought it on this trip or not. So much damned jewelry, she doesn't even know what she had."

"Who do you think did it?"

"Well, Rosen's got a bad temper and pops a few pints now and then. There's also the handyman, and there are the other guests. The sisters, Isabel in particular, were not that well liked."

"Hated is what I heard."

"Esther doesn't have any marks on her." Quinlan checked his notes. "It looks like the blood on her belongs to Isabel. The coroner will tell us more. Maybe they killed each other."

"Have you talked to anyone yet?" the Chief asked.

"Not yet. The Rosens aren't around. No one has seen them since this morning when they took their boat out. We're going to check all the boat ramps nearby. The handyman's in his room talking to Parkinson. The rest of the guests have been asked to stay in their rooms until we can talk to all of them. You know, of course that the Senator was a guest?"

"Stay away from that one, Mike. As far as we're concerned that will remain unsubstantiated." Chief Stevens had gotten the warning call from Phillips that pushed the right political buttons. Phillips warned the Chief to keep the Senator out of it.

"Anything you say, sir." Quinlan gave a mock salute.

"I expect regular reports on this one. It will be a hot press story and the sooner we have answers the better."

Quinlan bent down to take a look at an empty jewelry box. He grabbed one of the print specialists. "Can you get prints on this for me?" He looked further and spied a screwdriver next to the box.

"And print this one, too."

The car headlights from the police cruiser froze Buddy like a hypnotized animal on the highway.

"Hey, son, what are you doing out here?" the officer asked as he pulled up to Buddy and shined his flashlight on his face.

Buddy stared blankly at the policeman.

"Are you lost?"

"No," Buddy finally managed to say.

"Is that your bike there?" The officer shined the light on the bike that was lying at Buddy's feet.

"What's your name?"

"Um, Buddy ... Karl ... Rosen."

"Rosen?" He shined the light on Buddy's face again. "You related to Abe and Frances Rosen?"

"Uh huh. They're my parents."

"Come with us, son."

"Where?"

"To the police station, son. I think you may be more comfortable there ... until we get your parents for you." They helped Buddy into the cruiser and threw the bike into the trunk. The sky was darker than usual. There wasn't a star that shined that night.

"Max died," Buddy said after a few minutes on the road. He still looked hypnotized and dazed.

"What was that?" The officer asked.

"Max died. He was my friend. He was ... in the hospital."

"Did you visit Max?"

"Yes. Max had a lot of wires on him and he looked real bad. Is that why you arrested me? Because I sneaked into the hospital to see Max?"

"No, Buddy. You didn't do anything wrong."

"I killed him, you know."

Buddy laid down in the back seat and closed his eyes.

Ralph Jennings held little Audrey tight. The sweat drops poured from his head. "I told you, officer, Audrey wandered into the room because it was wide open. She didn't mean no harm. She came and got me right away. Then I called you guys."

Parkinson, the officer in charge of questioning, looked closely for any facial signs of lies. "Did you touch anything in the room, Jennings?"

"No, nothing."

"Did you, Audrey?"

"She didn't neither."

"Let her answer."

"She don't talk."

Parkinson bent down to look Audrey in the eyes. "Sweetie ... just nod yes or no ... did you touch anything?"

Audrey looked scared. She slowly nodded her head negatively back and forth. Parkinson made some notes in his book. Behind him there was a knock on the opened door.

"Ralph," Quinlan said as he let himself in. He looked around the room. He acknowledged Parkinson. "Mind if we look around?"

"Just a minute. You can't just come in and push me around like this."

"We have a search warrant, Ralph."

Jennings sat back down while two policemen went to work looking through his apartment for evidence. Audrey stroked her dolly's hair.

"What was it that you were in prison for, Ralph? "Parkinson asked.

"As if you don't know."

"Ralph, we only want to get at the truth."

"Then look for the killer. It ain't me. I don't have no reason to kill those ladies."

"How about robbery? Did they catch you red-handed?"

"I didn't do nothing. I already told you."

One of the policemen came up to Quinlan and whispered into his ear. "Excuse me." He followed the officer into the bedroom. He leaned down to look at the contents of a metal box that was sitting on the bed.

"Now, where do you suppose he got hold of a diamond ring like this?"

"There's more." The officer opened the door to another closet and brought out a cardboard box filled with money and a hunting knife.

"Book him."

RED HERRING:

Abe Reappears in an Unexpected Place

"Sal, we're going to be late." John Cabrera paced. He looked at his watch for the tenth time in five minutes. Why does she always do this? They were going be late for one of the most important days of their lives.

"I'm almost finished, John, just hold your horses." Sally yelled downstairs as she checked her hair in the mirror one more time. Just one more squirt of hair spray. Okay, now I'll just bet he'll offer to warm up the car, she thought.

"I'll go warm up the car, okay?"

"You do that, honey." Forty years of marriage counts for something. Forty years. Wow, it went by so quickly. That mirror can't be right. When did her hair turn that color? Hmmm, she thought, gotta make that appointment with the hairdresser soon.

Sally hit the lights and locked the front door.

"You look very pretty tonight, Sal." John kissed her as she let herself in the passenger side.

"Why, thank you, your honor. You look mighty dashing, yourself, in your new suit."Sally brushed his collar for imaginary lint. "Do you have your speech?"

He checked his pocket for his index cards. "Here it is." He pulled them out so fast that he dropped half of them on the seat. "Awww, man."

"I'll fix them. You just drive. It's going to be fine, just relax."

John put the car in gear and headed out of the driveway. "I don't know why I'm so nervous . It's not like I haven't sworn in judges before."

"You haven't sworn in your daughter before."

John glanced at Sally. "No, I haven't. That's true."

Mary never wanted for anything. She became the focus of excessive indulgence reserved for single-child families. There was, however, the time that the Cabrera family numbered four, including Audrey Jennings. Audrey was temporarily given a home with John, Sally and Mary after Ralph's arrest. Mary had been very fond of Audrey during their stay on the beach and she begged John and Sally to take care of her.

The decision was a difficult one.

It was the testiest year of their marriage. Sally had been unhappy with John's work schedule. He was pushing hard in those days to become partner. He had been given the most challenging clients and ungodly timetables. Their beach trip, which combined business and pleasure, was the first real semi-vacation they had since Mary was born. She had given up her career as a teacher to spend time with Mary, but was rethinking her decision.

John was worried about Sally. He realized that something was wrong, but couldn't quite grasp what it was. He knew she hated his schedule, but surely that was the only problem. That would be remedied as soon as he became partner, he thought. She was probably just bored. When Audrey needed a home,

John saw that as a perfect solution. It would be a great help to Audrey and a perfect way to "round out" the family and give Sally some new direction. Sally, of course, didn't see it that way at all.

There were bitter disagreements before Sally eventually consented to bringing Audrey home. Audrey was given a comfortable home, a new family and all the material things that her dad could never afford. But she never felt loved. John and Sally kept that guilt concealed for years afterward, but they never gave Audrey the love that she needed.

Mary loved Audrey. She worshiped her. Audrey just grew to resent Mary. She would always be "the only child" to her parents.

Audrey left home as soon as she turned 18.

John pulled into the parking lot and shut off the car. "Can you believe it? Can you believe our Mary is the newest circuit judge in Orleans Parish?" John puffed out his chest and pretended to smoke a cigar. "Where did we go wrong, Sal?"

Sally laughed. "I'll tell you this. I'm not going to call her your honor until she cleans out her closet. She is 38 years old. I think it's time, don't you?"

"Absolutely. I've been a judge for 20 years and I clean my closets," John winked.

"She's got your genes, honey. You only started to clean last year."

Bernie pulled into the K&B. His last fare was around the corner and the pain was getting worse. He needed to get some aspirin ... make that, extra, heavy, super sized aspirin.

He grabbed the one that had all the new and improved, more powerful garbage on the package.

"Headache, huh?" the cashier said, giving Bernie a dumb, acne-laden stare. He was all of eighteen years old and blinked a dozen times or so when Bernie just stared back at him. "That'll be two dollars and fifty three cents."

"Does that include the clinical diagnosis surcharge?" Bernie asked with a wicked sneer.

"The what? Um, no sir. There is no surcharge."

"Imagine that. And they say that health care providers like you are trying to squeeze every nickel out of the consumer."

"Not K&B. I can tell you that." The clerk leans closer to Bernie." Just between you and me, I wish they wouldn't squeeze so hard on the paychecks, though."

Bernie stepped back as the clerk broke into laughter. His head bobbed up and down as he chortled taking more air in than letting it out. Bernie was sure he'd pass out soon. At least he hoped he would.

Bernie grabbed the bag and pushed out the door. He tore opened the bottle and threw four pills in his mouth and swallowed hard. He pulled out a pint of Seagram's from under his seat and swigged it down.

"No more fares tonight," he thought to himself. He turned toward home, bypassing Lee Circle where two cabbies were shot just a week before. As he turned the corner, a man in a tuxedo stood directly in his path waving him down. He tried to swerve past him, but the man wouldn't let him.

Bernie pulled next to him and rolled down the window. "I'm off, mister. No more fares tonight."

"No. Please just take us to our house," John Cabrera was pleading to Bernie. "I'll pay you whatever you'd like. Just get us out of here. Our car stalled over there, and you are the first cab we've seen in over 20 minutes."

Sally was sitting in the car with her arms crossed, looking out the window, scowling.

"Well, you sure picked the wrong side of town to be stuck in."Bernie said as he looked around for signs of gangs.

"You're telling me."

"All right. Hop in."

John called to Sally who slowly walked to the cab and slid into her seat as John held open the door.

"Ma'am," Bernie nodded in Sally's direction. A courtesy nod was all that was given in return.

"We live at 1105 Melody Drive, are you familiar with Metairie?' John asked as he entered his side.

"Know it well." Bernie flipped the meter on and headed to the interstate. The pain crept down his back but was starting to dissipate slightly. The warmth of the pint still filled his belly.

"Are you going to continue to be angry, Sal?" John tried to move closer to Sally as she moved toward the door.

Sally made a face and motioned toward Bernie. "John, we'll talk about this at home."

Bernie tuned out the conversation. He was so used to chatter in the back seat, that he paid very little attention, unless it was something spicy that peeked his interest.

"I just want you to know that I never intended for that comment to be hurtful or demeaning in any way."

"Then why..." Sally stopped and whispered , "...why would you have even said it in the first place?"

"Stupidity. It was just stupidity, I guess."

"John, you're not a stupid man. Don't patronize me." Sally glanced toward Bernie again and lowered her voice, which had continued to rise. "I feel guilty enough about Audrey without you sharing it with 3,000 of your closest friends."

"But, Sal, I didn't even use her name. Sam was telling the story about his two kids so I ..."

"... had to talk about Audrey."

"No ... I agreed. I was just giving a metaphorical example, using our experience as a way to tell how close our love for Mary was and how difficult it is when ... you know ... when there is another child in the house. As much as we tried and wanted to love Audrey the same, our daughter was still number one. I'm sure other parents feel the same with foster children in the same house." John tried again to move closer.

"Audrey Jennings was not our child," Sally said in a voice louder than she wanted it to be. She burst into tears and fell onto John's shoulder.

Suddenly, Bernie's interest was piqued. A name from the past: Little Audrey Jennings. Ironic that they too had an Audrey Jennings in their lives as well. Even more ironic that it should happen on the day that he finally took out the old films that he hadn't watched in more than 30 years.

Sally continued through her tears. "That poor child. She had been through so much. She just wanted to be loved. She lost her father, she lost her home .... Mary loved her, though."

John added: "I wish we knew what happened to her. If only she could have been there to see Mary. I know Mary wished she could have been there too."

Bernie started to think about Audrey and Ralph. He started to think about Frannie and Buddy, too. He didn't miss Abe. Abe died just like the press clips said he did. Bernie was born at the same time.

It had been so long ago but the feelings were as strong today as they were then. The pain in his back wasn't even a fraction of the pain he felt over his guilt and sorrow about his family.

"You were a good mother, Sally, a good mother to both our children." John rubbed her arm and her shoulder.

"And you were a good father ... still a good father, John. You were the one that took Audrey in. You were the one that gave her a voice ..."

Bernie listened.

"... you replaced that hideous doll without arms with wonderful toys ..."

He froze. Bernie looked into the rearview window. "Who the hell's in my cab?" He thought as he scanned their faces for signs of recognition. The man does look familiar.

John rocked Sally gently in the back seat. "She was so upset when old Ralph committed suicide in his jail cell. I think she felt like he would come back for her one day ..."

Bernie had read the press clips. Ralph got the short end. It figured. Guys like Ralph and him always get the short end. Ralph just pushed ahead of schedule. Bernie would wait until his liver is eaten away.

"You remember the guy who ran that place? The ... um ... Palms?" John questioned.

Nausea overtook Bernie. He couldn't be sure if it was his gut acting up or the shock of getting thrown back to the past.

"Mr. Rosen — Abe Rosen. He and his wife died in that boat accident, right?" Sally asked.

"Right. Well, you know Schneider, my Tampa Bay client?

"Uh huh."

“He was telling me about this teacher his grandson has and what unusual methods he uses with the students … like old home movies and reading lofts and math castles and stuff … well, turns out that the teacher is Buddy Rosen. I recognized the name and asked if he had anything to do with the Palms Motel. Schneider says his old man owned the place. That’s Abe’s son. He’s teaching in St. Petersburg.”

Bernie swerved as an oncoming car almost hit them. His ears were ringing. He felt completely numb.

“Whoa. That was a close one,” John said to Bernie.

“Oh … sorry. It’s just one of those teenagers out cruising. Are you two all right?” Bernie asked.

“I think so. Thank you,” Sally answered.

“Gets a little crazy at night downtown, huh?” John asked.

“Sure does. You from New Orleans or just visiting?” Bernie glanced at John and Sally in the rearview mirror.

John moved closer to Bernie’s ear. “Born and raised. Just don’t get downtown too often any more.”

Bernie strained to look at John closer in the mirror. His memory was getting so bad. He recognized the face, but he could have known him in New Orleans. His clientele at the Palms were faded memories.

“Have you lived here long?” John asked Bernie.

“Thirty years.”

“Long enough to call you a y’at.”

“Speaking of that … guess where y’at.” Bernie pulled up to the curb of 1105 Melody Drive.

John laughed and patted Bernie on the shoulder. “That was very good, Mister … ?”

"Abraham. Bernie Abraham." Bernie shook hands with John as he opened his door. "I didn't catch your name."

"Cabrera. I'm John and my wife's Sally." Sally grimaced as John introduced her. She hated when he was so open to strangers and told them all about their personal lives. That's twice tonight. First, he told the story of Audrey to the entire party and now he gives the cabbie his name. Next he'll tell him the combination to the safe.

John glanced at the meter and handed Bernie a fifty. Bernie looked at the bill. "I don't know if I can cash this, let me check."

"No need to, Mr. Abraham, it's yours. Thank you so much for your help." Sally sighed and mumbled to herself.

"Thanks, Mr. Cabrera. Here's my card. If you need transportation any time, just call this number."

Bernie jumped back in the cab. His mind was swimming. John Cabrera. It was coming back to him. He was on a business trip. His wife was a pain in the ass. He wondered for a brief minute if Cabrera recognized him. Fat chance, he thought as he looked in the mirror. His face had dramatically changed since he got sick. The yellowed pallor in his cheeks ... hell, he didn't even have cheeks any more. He looked a good 10 years older than he was. His eyelids were drooping so low, he thought. He could use them as baseball gloves. So, what if he did recognize him? At this point, he was almost dead. He couldn't be killed twice.

Maybe it was time.

Bernie was 30 minutes late.

Wayne Petagna grew impatient. He sat with the chess set

primed for the next move. Their weekly matches were in their second decade. Wayne won thirteen times. He remembered each one. He also remembered the losses, all 459 of them. His years of employment as a bank teller gave him a real penchant for data and his lifelong feeling of inadequacy gave him a penchant for ulcers.

They were a pair. Bernie with his liver and Wayne with his stomach. Wayne spent most of his adult life on a toilet seat, while Bernie spent most of his on a barstool. Wayne was Bernie's first friend when he came to New Orleans. In fact, it was Wayne who got him his first loan to buy a cab. In a moment of weakness, Bernie invited Wayne out to celebrate. By the time they hit the third strip bar at about midnight, Wayne was spending more time in the john than at the bar. Bernie, of course, was numb to any pain and wound up on the street after trying to dance with one of the more vocal strippers. They stuck with chess, it was easier on both of them.

"Hey, Stuff." Bernie shuffled in and pulled up the chair opposite Wayne. He called him Stuff because of his stuffy ways. Wayne took pride in it, though. He chose to think that it related to big stuff.

"Bernie," Wayne said kept his chin up and looked down his nose at the chess set.

"Aww. Are you mad at me honey. I didn't call?"

"Fuck you, Bernie."

"Obscenities? Why, Wayne, I am very impressed."

"Let's just play."

"Okay. Okay. But I gotta tell you something, Stuff."

Wayne raised his head in a bored manner. "What?"

"One of my fares last night talked to each other about Abe Rosen and actually stayed at the Palms ... the day I left."

Wayne looked around the room and then leaned in. He was the only human being that knew that Bernie was Abe. It had taken many years and about five shots one night for Bernie to tell Wayne his secret. "Did you know them?"

"Yes. No. Well kinda. I remember them but only vaguely."

"Did they recognize you?

"Are you kidding? Look at me, Stuff. Do I look like I did even 10 years ago?"

"Well ..."

"You don't have to be kind. I look like shit."

"Okay, you look like shit and not a thing like you did 10 years ago."

"Thanks ... I think."

"So, do you think you're safe?"

Bernie leaned back in his chair and put his hands behind his head. "I don't really care."

"What? Are you crazy, Bernie? They are probably still looking for you. You could get killed."

"So? I've been dead for a long time, anyway. I just never fell down. I've lived like this for more than 30 years, Stuff, not that I didn't deserve it. Maybe now is the time."

"The time for what?"

"The time for me to return to the scene."

"Bernie, are you sure?"

"No. But I've never been sure about anything in my life, so I wouldn't want to start that kind of policy now. I am pretty sure about one thing, though. I want to see my son before I die. And there are some old scores to settle."

Wayne studied Bernie's face. He looked calm tonight. Even his face started to look a little younger. Music filled the restaurant as they sat looking at each other. Dr. John sang "Just A Closer Walk With Thee," and Bernie closed his eyes, humming the melody.

"You know, if I were Buddy, I'd probably beat the shit out of Abe ... that is, if he wants to even see the man who killed his mother and then left without even looking back." Bernie talked in the third person about Abe. He separated himself from that persona completely, Wayne thought. It was too painful.

"When I woke up on that boat, I had only one thought. To save my ass. I knew that I'd either get it from the cops, the SOBs or the guy I must have pissed off that tried to kill me."

Bernie looked out the window and saw a street vendor selling flowers on the corner. He started to tear up. "God, I miss Frannie."

"When you first told me about what you did, Bernie, I was shocked." Wayne leaned on the table and knocked the king down. He reached over and put it in the box. "I wanted to turn you in. Even though we were friends, I just couldn't live with my conscience."

"Why didn't you?"

"Because, I started to think about it. You were in prison in your mind for so long and you had lost all that you loved. Your punishment continued." Wayne stopped as his stomach turned flips a few times. "But the main reason was your son."

"Buddy?"

"Yes, Buddy. He thought you and his mother died in a boating accident. He would have to know the truth and live with that the rest of his life. I wasn't sure that I wanted to be responsible for that. That, my friend, is your decision to make."

"I know, Wayne. I know."

"When do you leave?"

"Tomorrow."

Wayne put the rest of the chess game in the box and closed the lid. He stood up and motioned for Bernie to join him. "Let's get drunk."

"Fuckin' A!"

PLOT POINT:

Unexplained Murder and a Blast From the Past

Roger Phillips turned his collar up to block the wind. He crossed Broadway and ducked into a little coffee shop. He sat at the counter and ordered a black coffee ... hot.

"A little chilly, are we?" The counter waitress asked. Phillips tried to figure out what nationality she was. Chinese, Japanese, Vietnamese or some other "ese," he thought to himself. New York has been completely overrun with Indians and Chinese ... where are the white Americans?

"Yeah. Forty degrees chilly. "

Phillips hated the city. He only moved here because of his wife. She decided that New York City was where her new career could flourish. Well, truth be known, she had no new career ... she wanted one.

She ... was Ann English.

Ann English (Jimenez) latched on to Phillips right after Jimmy Bennett died ... literally after Bennett died. Bennett had a massive heart attack in the middle of a final thrust into and on top of English. Phillips, as always, was right outside.

He remembered that night well.

Bennett was being honored as the Man of the Year by the Florida Chamber of Commerce and the SOB Foundation. He came dressed to kill, white tuxedo and all. Mrs. Bennett was squeezed into a tight fitting white dress with a plunging neckline that accented her ample cleavage as well as the ample rolls of skin under her arms and on her back.

They sat at the head table next to Oscar and Ramon Martinez and their wives. Bennett was full of bluster.

"Oscar ... this is our night. I know my name is on the award, but it really belongs to both of us."

Martinez patted Bennett on the shoulder. "Jimmy, you are the true Man of the Year. It wouldn't have happened without you."

"Thank you, Oscar. I know that my efforts were important. Probably the critical pressure points to get things rolling ... and I did spend many days pushing for funding from all fronts ... but you and your people have protected our shores for many years." Bennett raised his glass. "I'd like to propose a toast."

Everyone raised their glasses.

"Here's to all the SOBs that keep our beaches beautiful and here's to me ... Man of the Year!" He burst out laughing while everyone took a sip of their champagne.

Anna was sitting at a table off to the side with a few political wannabes sucking up to Phillips. The Klemwiches were on his right bending his ear about the plumbing business and how the state is destroying small businesses by imposing unprecedented tax hikes. Harvey Sheppard was on his left bemoaning the high cost of medical insurance that he has to pay for his five employees at his hardware store. Both claimed to be big contributors to Bennett's reelection campaign.

"The senator truly appreciates your support and I will certainly tell him about your concerns for our state." He wanted to say ... you really think he gives a shit about your $100 contribution and your stupid whining?

Bennett texted Phillips: "Find me a room I can use for about an hour."

(For God sake ... can't you keep it in your pants until you make your speech?) "I'll check," was Phillips reply.

He excused himself from the table and went to the front desk. He approached a very well-dressed and very gay clerk.

"Pardon me. I was wondering if you had a room available?"

"For tonight?"

(No ... for an hour.) "Yes, please."

"Let me check ..." His fingers raced across the keyboard making it seem like he was writing the entire Declaration of Independence to search for one room. "Ahhh ... wait ... no ... that one is taken ... let me try another." This time it was more like the first thirty chapters of Moby Dick.

Phillips checked his watch. It was getting close to the time that the program was going to start.

"Here we go ... there is a premium king on the second floor ..."

"Good. I'll take it."

"I just need a credit card ..."

"Here. Keep the card. I'll be back for it." Phillips grabbed the key and ran to the ballroom.

He caught Anna's eye and motioned her to join him outside. He watched her as she smiled to the table guests and excused herself. God, she was beautiful. He never tired of watching her and he longed for every opportunity to be alone with her.

"Room 236." He handed her the key. "I'll get The Man of the Year and he'll meet you upstairs."

Anna scurried to the elevator as Phillips slipped into the ballroom and scribbled the number on a piece of paper. He made his way to the head table. No mistaking Phillips when he walked. He moved like a mouse. He was tiny and skinny and skittered about like he was caught in a maze. He approached Bennett, handed him a note and looked solemn.

"Sorry, dear," Bennett said to his wife. "Important call I must take."

"Oh ... Jimmy ... you are speaking in about 45 minutes."

"I'll be back in plenty of time."

He never made it back to the table.

Phillips paid two bellmen to pick him up in a wheelchair and prop him in a stall. They used the service elevator and managed to get him there undetected.

It was Phillips who "found" him after a few minutes and informed his wife. What a shame; he died on a toilet at the Plaza Hotel.

Anna lost her meal ticket when Bennett died and Phillips was there to offer another. He didn't have the standing that the Senator had but he did have quite a lot of money.

And Anna was all about comfort.

Phillips was tired of politics. He still had his political connections and still retained his attachment to the Sons of the Beaches. He proudly wore his ring. He and Anna made regular visits to The Palms over the next few years and he was often in the center of Foundation business as an advisor and a donor. He also served for a while as the Foundation Counsel.

He and Anna got married on St. Pete Beach. Oscar Martinez was his best man. Oscar never really cared for Phillips. He never trusted him and thought that he gave Bennett bad advice when he was still alive. Ramon, on the other hand, liked Phillips. He felt that there was much that he could learn from him in business and politics.

On the other hand, Ramon did not have a great deal of love for his father. He thought him a weak man. There were important issues that Oscar would turn away from, Ramon thought. Phillips was fearless and cunning ... two traits that intrigued Ramon. It was really Phillips who got Ramon interested and involved in the Sons of the Beaches Foundation, not Oscar.

Ramon had seen the Foundation as a dead end until Phillips had shown him that foundations can be quite lucrative if the funding model is tweaked. And he knew just how to do it.

It was Phillips who put together the land use plan that provided the shared property arrangement with the Palms and the Foundation, which provided benefits for both. Abe's will was vague and unclear as to who inherited the property. Buddy was still a teenager and the other family members had no real interest. By blending the properties and making the mission a shared SOB determining factor, the Martinez family became the beneficiary and the income from the Palms was run through Foundation books.

Expansion of the Palms became an important part of the fundraising mission of the SOB Foundation and created a new entity that produced greater income. Oscar Martinez ran the operation until he died at 87. Ramon was named manager and eventually director of the Foundation.

Buddy Rosen came to Oscar's funeral.

He had been away for a long time ... a lifetime ago. Oscar was a link to his past ... a friend of his father's. His passing was a few years before the passing of his Aunt Selma, the woman who raised him and filled the void left when his mother and father died.

Selma was a strong, loving woman who never once hesitated in her role as Buddy's second mother. She stepped right up when Abe and Frances were presumed dead and proudly took on her new role.

Selma's last few years were very difficult.

She had developed ovarian cancer, which had not been diagnosed until it had advanced to a terminal stage. Selma was fighting for her life for three long years. She was Buddy's only family and he was losing her.

During these dark days, a light appeared in his life.

Andi Fenimore came into his classroom and into his life on the first day of school. She was trying to find her classroom and accidentally stepped into the kindergarten classroom. It was pitch black and when she tried to feel around to find the switch, she fell into the Math Castle and knocked over an entire shelf of comic books.

Buddy jumped up and turned on the lights. He was wearing flannel pajamas and she was laying spread eagle under fifty issues of Spiderman. They both looked at each other and burst out laughing.

"I am so, so sorry," Andi said still laughing. "I must be in the wrong ... are those pajamas?"

"Yes, they are. This is nap time ... and you are very close to having a snake in your hair." Voltaire's cage was teetering right over her head.

"Oh my God .... oh my God ... it really is ..." Andi started to scramble around to get up.

"Stop!" She froze.

"Okay ... just stop right there and I'll fix the cage ... if you move, it might come down." Buddy straightened up the cage and put Voltaire back in his cubby.

Bob Kevin came in the door. "Hey ... what's the racket here? I'm trying to sleep next door."

"I'm sorry," Andi said. "It was my fault. You were having nap time too?"

"No. I teach sixth grade. I just sleep a lot." Kevin helped her up. "I'm Bob Kevin."

Andi rose to her feet. At this point the entire kindergarten class was on their feet too. "Andi Fenimore."

Buddy had not stopped staring at Andi since she got there.

Kevin finally said, "He's Rosen ... Buddy Rosen ... Mr. Chivalry."

Buddy finally snapped out of it. "Oh ... I'm so sorry." He grabbed her hand and shook it erratically. "Nice to meet you."

Andi said, "Do you know where the Art Classroom is?"

"Ah u an ahtist?" Joshua Ferguson asked.

"Um ... yes I am." Andi smiled . "Are you?"

"I'm a Pwesbeterian."

"Okay," Buddy said, trying not to laugh too hard. "Everybody back to bed. Nap time is over in fifteen minutes."

Eventually, Andi made it to her classroom and into Buddy Rosen's heart. There were things about Andi ... familiar things that made him comfortable. Her confident smile hid her vulnerability and made her even more interesting to be around. He shared intimate secrets with her that he didn't share with anyone else.

She knew of his nightmares, of his fears, of his past loves ... and his past failures. He told her about his drinking and about his aggression. No one — even Kevin — knew the things he shared.

Andi didn't share much about her life at all. He knew she lost her father too and that she had a rough life ... but she didn't share and he didn't ask.

He didn't have to.

Phillips left the coffee shop and stepped into the chilled air once again.

He was headed home. Anna would not be there. She had packed her things and was off to hook up with her next millionaire. There was a note waiting for Roger Phillips. Simple and direct: "Sorry, darling, I have met someone else. I don't have the courage to tell you to your face. I'm such a coward. Please forgive me. Love, Anna."

Phillips stopped at a flower shop. He loved to get Anna white roses ... picked them up on the first of every month. Today, he found yellow roses and bought a dozen to surprise her. She often complained that he was not very spontaneous. This would help change that.

He headed for the Broadway/7th Ave. Station, the same one he took every day to go home. Off hours were so much better, he thought. Not many trashy people to deal with. He could afford a taxi but ... he liked saving the money and the trip was a short one. The only other passenger in the station was sitting to his right on a bench reading a paper. He sat in the shadows but looked vaguely familiar. Oh well, he thought as he looked down at the flowers, Anna will be very impressed.

In the distance, he saw the single light of the train coming toward him. He stepped to the edge. It happened in an instance. Phillips felt a strong kick in the middle of his back, causing him to fly off the platform and land headfirst on the rails.

He was dead before the train cut him in half.

SET-UP:

Buddy Survives and Chrissy Learns the Rest of the Story

Detective Michael Quinlan stood over the sleeping figure of Buddy Rosen. There were lines attached to monitors and tubes coming from every visible orifice on Rosen's body.

Quinlan hated hospitals. The depressive atmosphere, the smells, the loss of control both physically and mentally brought back unpleasant memories of the times that he spent as a patient himself. Too much time. There were numerous surgeries to repair bones that were crushed and broken in his pelvis, his hips and legs. Pins and orthopedic devices held together joints that were shattered by a car crash that almost took his life.

He worked homicide for 28 years. Before that, he was a street cop for 8 years. He had worked the tough cases.

There was the plumber who chopped up his customers and stuffed them into the sewer systems. Quinlan wasn't in charge of that one, but he did come up with the key evidence, a bloodstained toolbox hidden under the floorboards in the plumber's truck. Then there was the Reinhold Case. Mrs. Reinhold was a loving wife and mother who got rid of her husband by getting her kids to push him off their boat.

Quinlan got a teary confession from the younger son on the anniversary of his father's death. But the case that really became the turning point in his career involved two brothers, Billy and Gary Barody. Drugs and politics were the catalyst that set the brothers into a tailspin of violence that ended in the murders of two city councilmen and a judge. The crucial evidence in the case were microscopic blood particles on Billy Barody's shoes and subsequent phone calls by both brothers, all uncovered by Quinlan after many nights of dangerous stakeouts.

Mike Quinlan flashed back to the day that he had to give Buddy the news that his parents were gone ... that Abe's boat was found in the Gulf ... drifting far from land without its passengers.

It was too much for Buddy, who was still in shock over the death of his friend Max. He spent weeks in the hospital. The doctors were not sure if he would ever be the same.

Quinlan was laden with guilt. He felt responsible for Buddy's deep depression. And at the same time, he carried the additional burden of a secret affair ... with Frances Rosen.

After that ... his life changed.

He pulled out his portable tape recorder and read aloud the messages and get-well cards that were scattered around the room. "Some of Buddy's admirers, I guess," he dictated, "... 'You are in our prayers, Much Love, Linda Rankin' ...'We miss you, the Kindergarten class' ... 'Helluva way to get out of paying your bar tab, We love ya Buddy Boy, Debbie' and ... hmmm, can't make out the last one ..."

"... Manny," A voice answered weakly.

"What?" Quinlan looked around for the person who answered.

"Manny ... his name is Manny." Buddy looked up at Quinlan as the fog started to clear. "Hey, Quinlan!"

"Well look who just woke up."

"Pardon me for not getting up to shake hands, Michael," Buddy tried to sit up but felt dizzy. "There's this hole in my chest."

"I tried to teach you not to play with guns." Quinlan sat down on the bed next to Buddy.

"Yeah? Well you did a shitty job, I guess." Buddy said a few indecipherable words and dropped off to sleep.

A nurse swept past to check the IV and note the chart. "Sir, I think it would be wise to let Mr. Rosen rest for a while." She gently pushed Detective Quinlan out the door of the intensive care unit.

"Is the doc around?" Quinlan asked.

"Doctor Price is in surgery until 3:00," the nurse replied.

"Will you tell him I was here? I just have a few questions." Quinlan handed the nurse one of his cards.

"I will."

Quinlan put his wallet in his inside coat pocket and headed quickly down the hospital corridor. Chrissy Rosen didn't see him coming as she rounded the corner to Buddy's room. They collided, knocking Chrissy to the floor and Michael against the wall.

"Damn," Chrissy said as she started to get up. "Why don't you watch where you are going ?"

Quinlan bent down to pick her up. When he extended his hand, his jacket opened and his gun was exposed. Chrissy immediately jumped back and tried to run away.

Quinlan realized she saw the gun and grabbed her arm. "I'm a police detective."

"That's a relief," Chrissy said as she settled down. "I thought maybe you were ... well anyway, you're not."

He looked at the mess of papers that Chrissy dropped when she fell. "Let me help you."

"That's okay. I can get them."

But Quinlan had already started to pick them up. He stopped to read one of the pages. It was a get-well letter from one of Buddy's students, written in black crayon and illustrated with a colorful picture of Buddy in bed with a thermometer as big as his arm coming out of his mouth. It read: "Git wll Mistr Rosun. We miss u. lov, valerie".

"Do you mind?!" Chrissy said indignantly as she grabbed the letter out of his hands.

"Are these for Buddy Rosen?" Quinlan asked.

"Yes. Do you know him?"

"Since he was just a little shit ... um, kid. I'm investigating the shooting. The name's Michael Quinlan." He held out his hand. Reluctantly, Chrissy shook it.

"I'm Christina Rosen."

"Are you his wife?"

"No. I happen to be his daughter. You're really some detective, huh?"

"That's what my badge says."

"I'm sure."

"Listen, I know you've been through a lot, but I wonder if you could give me a call after you visit your dad." He handed Chrissy a card.

She grabbed it. Chrissy started to rush down the hall toward his room but stopped in mid stride and turned. "Detective Quinlan?"

"Yes."

"Do you know who did this?"

"Not yet, but it's probably not a close personal friend."

Chrissy smiled and turned to walk away. "Brilliant," she remarked in a whisper.

"On the other hand, it was no stranger."

Chrissy turned back again. "How do you know that?"

"We found the gun. It belonged to your dad."

Chrissy felt physically and emotionally drained by the time she got back to the house. There wasn't a muscle in her body that didn't cry out for help. She was grateful that Andi had come by to relieve her at the hospital.

Buddy was getting a little better. The signs looked promising. Dr. Price had given orders to keep Buddy in the intensive care unit a few more days.

Chrissy loaded the dishes into the dishwasher and turned on the switch. Her whole world had turned upside down. Her dad had been shot down in the street. She was scared. Thoughts of death filled her mind ... her own death. Was she in danger? Who tried to kill her father ... would they try to kill her?

She always worried about her father. Even in her darkest days — when her mother packed her up and moved back to New York — she could think only about her father. They had a relationship unlike any other.

They shared so many traits.

Buddy had treated Chrissy like an adult from the time she was a little girl. His sense of humor was never lost on her. Wise cracking had been part of her DNA.

Janet didn't get it; she never did. The little inside jokes were insulting to her, even demeaning at times. It didn't matter that they weren't talking about her. She was upset that they didn't include her. The stupid way they laughed when no one else knew what they were laughing about always drove her crazy.

It came to a head when they moved. Janet had made it clear where she stood.

"Mom," Chrissy said as Janet unpacked in the new apartment, "Do you think Daddy will be lonely without us?"

"Chrissy," Janet said with tears in her eyes. "This is the beginning of our new life. I don't want to discuss it again. He will always be your father and I'm sure will always love you — but starting today, it is you and I."

"But who is going to take care of him?"

"He will find another sidekick, I'm sure."

Chrissy called him secretly to check on him. Janet would have had a fit if she knew. Every call would end with the same question. "Chrissy, how's your mom? Does she talk about me?" Chrissy and Buddy began making up comedy routines (which was such a relief for her ... she hated to lie to her father about Janet's true feelings).

There was a boy in her life. Not anymore ... not for a long time.

Stanley Michael Cohen was an accountant at one of the big firms in Manhattan. He was actually doing an internship but she always introduced him using all three of his names and referred to his "position" at Graham, Bullard and Bernstein. Funny, Chrissy wasn't really big on prestige but somehow felt that Stan needed that — and she was going to do that for him.

She met Stan at Princeton when she was taking an accounting class and he was the graduate assistant. She hated that class. It was one of the requirements she needed to finish her pre-law degree. Stan was intrigued by her; actually he was in love with her from the first day they met. He knew she was struggling with the class and carefully planned his first move to get to know her.

It was at the library.

Stan followed her every week and planted himself at a table directly behind and to the right of hers. He was just out of range for her to notice him but right in range for him to see her.

It took weeks to get up the courage but he eventually did. He slowly wandered up to her table, sweat dripping beneath his armpits under his sweater. "Hi."

Chrissy looked up and after a very uncomfortable pause finally said "hello."

"You're ... Chrissy Rosen."

Chrissy closed her book with a flourish and stood facing him. "You've been stalking me for six weeks and that's the best you can come up with Stanley?"

Stan swallowed hard and turned red.

Chrissy continued, "Well, what else do you have to say for yourself?"

Stan finally caught his breath. "Please don't call me Stanley. Only my mother and the three kids that beat me up in the third grade called me that."

It was so unexpected that Chrissy laughed out loud … and so did Stan. "Would you like to sit down, Mr. Cohen, and teach me the hidden secrets about Accounting 101?"

"Sure. I would be happy to."

He was so different. She usually went for the athletes. Not necessarily big and stupid … big and … well … pretty stupid. She was athletic and was always drawn to those that she could "do stuff" with. It helped that they all had incredible abs — but Stan was definitely different.

He was actually smart and he didn't talk about himself at all.

Unlike a lot of her Princeton friends, Stan came from a middle-class Jewish family in Hoboken. His dad was an accountant with a small firm and his mother was a piano teacher.

He shared that bit of information with Chrissy on their fifth "study date." They were sharing a pitcher at one of the bars on Nassau Street. Stan drew out his family tree on a napkin. He was just getting to the branch that held his great Uncle Saul when Chrissy grabbed the napkin and put it in his beer mug. "Stan, I only asked what your father did for a living."

"I thought you might be interested in …"

"I am. But right now I'm more interested in the cute little dimple on your chin."

"This one?" Stan pointed to the indent.

"Yeah. That one."

"You know … my Uncle Morris had a dimple in the same place. His father had a cleft right there …"

Chrissy planted a big wet kiss right on Stan's lips. "That's the only way to get you to shut up. Let's go to my place."

A week later they were sharing more than accounting tips and a wet kiss here and there. They were roommates and Chrissy was happier than she had ever been in her life.

That next semester, Stan started his internship and got a small apartment in Soho. Chrissy came in for weekends and juggled a busy schedule. Her plan was to finish her year at Princeton, maybe go to Columbia Law School and then ... they would see.

It was a Friday, Chrissy remembered. She had no classes and she would surprise Stan. They never get long weekends. Always worried about school, she could finally relax.

She got to the apartment early so she could make a big dinner and have it ready for him when he got home. The surprise belonged to Chrissy.

He was home ... so was another intern that worked with him ... Barry. Alas, Stanley had a new "love" in his life.

She hadn't seen him since. It had been two years.

Chrissy realized that she hadn't even called her mom since she'd been there. Janet had left her three messages. She picked up the phone to dial the number but changed her mind at the last second. She dialed the hospital instead.

"Andi?"

"Hi, Chrissy," Andi answered.

"How's Daddy doing ?"

"Fine."

"Any changes?"

"Not yet, honey. He's still resting comfortably."

"Have you seen the doctor?"

"He stopped by a few minutes ago just to say hi."

"Oh."

"Are you okay, Chrissy?"

"Sure, I'm fine. Andi. Thanks."

"You just try to get some rest. Okay?"

"Uh huh."

Chrissy hung up the phone and sat on the counter.

She looked down at the trashcan. It was overflowing with neglect. There was still broken glass from the picture of Abe and Frances. There also was the card she got from Detective Quinlan.

"What the hell!"

She dialed his number.

It was close to sundown. Quinlan sat across from Chrissy at one of the picnic styled tables on the patio of the Hurricane Restaurant. Since he was off duty, he drank a beer while she sipped on a glass of water that felt like it weighed a hundred pounds in her hands. She started to relax as the warm breeze from the gulf hit her face. She startled a little as the speakers blared with the traditional announcement and drumroll as the sun started to sink. Despite her state of distress, she suddenly laughed out loud.

"What's so funny?" Quinlan asked.

Chrissy couldn't stop giggling as heads turned around to look. "It's the prerecorded sunset. It's a perfect end to a totally unreal day — week — life!"

"You know I'm so used to the 'sound system' sunsets here that I don't pay any attention to them anymore."

Chrissy looked out at the water. "I wish I would have grown up here on the beach. Look at those kids." Two little sandy, brown, wet toddlers carefully squeezed wet dripping sand through their fingers over their sand castle creation. A third looked on with hands on hips and back arched, admiring their creation. "They look so happy, so normal, building their dream castle. It's a shame that it will be gone in the morning."

"The nice thing about a sandcastle is that it can always be rebuilt."

"But it won't ever look the same."

"Is that important?"

"I always thought so." Chrissy couldn't stop looking at the kids who now danced around the castle then ran into the water.

The waiter leaned in. "Can I get you anything else?"

"Hmm?" Chrissy broke her stare. "Oh, no thanks."

"Not hungry?" asked Quinlan as Chrissy nodded, no. "Well I am. I think I'll have the blackened grouper sandwich and another one of these." He pointed to his empty beer glass.

"Coming right up." The waiter grabbed the empty and hustled to another table.

"Oh, look," Chrissy said as she sat upright, "that must be the daddy. He's standing guard over the castle as the kids swim."

"Bet you're right." Quinlan smiled as he glanced at the man who crossed his arms and stood watching the kids. "You know I hear your dad's real popular with kids."

"Yes, he is. He's a great teacher. He's very funny, enjoys teaching, enjoys the kids and they enjoy him."

"Was he always a teacher?"

"Yep, as long as I can remember. It was his life. He'd have these big ideas for his class in the middle of the night. He'd wake me up and ask me what I thought about a Roman forum with kids playing the members of the senate or cooking his famous hot chili for a math lesson on counting the ingredients. That one I told him was a dumb idea. His chili was horrible.

"My friends would tease me a lot. I never was embarrassed about the fact that he was a teacher. But, sometimes I pretended he wasn't related to me when we were on campus. Wasn't cool, you know. Once, he called my name really loudly across the quadrangle. I was talking to a cute boy and he knew I'd be embarrassed. So … he yelled, 'Chrissy, daddy loves you!' I could have killed him!"

"Dads have a talent for embarrassment," Quinlan said.

"Yeah. Mine's very talented. And very abnormal."

Chrissy stared out to look for the kids on the beach. They were nowhere to be seen only the castle remained. Out of the corner of her eye, Chrissy spotted a couple of teens playing frisbee. One was running full speed toward the castle, his eyes over his shoulder following the disc as it floated in his direction. He caught it on his fingertips just as his foot smashed through the castle walls. Chrissy sighed.

"Chrissy …"

The waiter interrupted, "Here we go: grouper and a beer. Are you sure you don't want anything?" He looked at Chrissy.

"No thanks," Chrissy said as the waiter smiled and scribbled on the check. He disappeared into the crowd.

Quinlan continued, "Chrissy, why did you call? Do you have information that is vital to the case? If so, I need to look at it."

Chrissy looked out at the remains of the sand castle and quietly sobbed. "I don't know what to do. I'm worried about my dad. There are pieces to my life that are missing and I can't put them together. I feel like my life is inside that sand castle …"

Quinlan reached for her hand, but Chrissy pulled it away. "Look. How about if I tell you what I know. You need to hear the story, anyway."

Chrissy felt the fear.

"Your grandfather, Abe, was, well, he was not a nice man. He was known to be abusive to your father and to your grandmother. He hit the bottle pretty regularly. I was called more than once to settle a family disturbance."

"Daddy told me about that."

"But, that wasn't the worst of it," Quinlan continued. "Abe was also involved with some pretty powerful men."

"Mobsters?"

"Worse. They were politicians and businessmen. There was a case I worked 30 years ago that really became a media circus. It involved two brothers, Billy and Gary Barody. They had a government contract for the new roadwork that was going to link the beaches with the city. They lost the contract to a company from Tampa. The brothers turned to violence. It ended in the murders of two city councilmen and a judge. The crucial evidence in the case were microscopic blood particles on Billy Barody's shoes and phone calls from the Palms Motel. They were never attributed to Abe but his business associations with the Barodys were legendary."

"Was he ever arrested?"

"No. He came close a few times, tiptoed around some petty crimes like minor assault, theft and drunkenness. I was always suspicious of the major stuff. Then he showed his true colors." Quinlan took a picture out of his pocket and showed it to Chrissy.

"I recognize Abe, but who's the other guy grinning?"

"That's Senator James Bennett, known in his younger days as the Road Hog. He was the chairman of the Transportation Committee and was a favorite with contractors who generously rewarded him."

"Like the Barody Brothers?"

"Like the Barody Brothers. Your grandfather 'hosted' many of the Senator's weekend retreats at the Palms and had his Palms greased a few times for it."

"Frances knew ..."

"Yes. Your grandmother was going to leave him and turn state's evidence."

"I think ... we found it."

"I know. It was all in Buddy's trunk when we searched his car."

"So you knew. So Abe ..."

"... killed Frances. He was killed too, probably by one of the senator's goons and covered up by a boating accident."

"But Abe's still ..." Chrissy froze. Does Quinlan know about the films?

"... alive? No. The movie of Abe is probably a fake." Quinlan noticed Chrissy's creased brow. "Yes, I know about the movies. We found them too."

"How? How do you fake something like that?"

"Electronic imaging, processing, using old movies and replacing the face; it's not hard to do anymore."

"Why would someone want us to think that Abe was alive?"

"I don't know. I thought maybe you could tell me that."

"Me? I couldn't even tell you my name at this point."

"What can you tell me about the safety deposit box?"

"I thought you had all of it."

"Most of it — were there other documents?"

"Well, there was this that my dad gave me ... to hold." Chrissy pulled out her bag and took out the contents. She handed him the package, "And I'll be happy to give you these. I've been nervous carrying them around."

Quinlan carefully unwrapped the black velvet pouch. He looked inside and let out a laugh dropping them onto the table in front of him.

"I'm glad to see you enjoy your work so much, Detective."

"It's Esther's missing jewelry. I recognize the bag. You see? It's got her initials on it." Quinlan burst into laughter again.

"That's funny?"

"They're fakes."

"Costume jewelry? She kept costume jewelry in a black velvet bag?"

"She wanted everyone to think they were real."

Chrissy felt that burning flushed feeling again. "Well, I'll tell you what's real. My father's got a bullet hole in him. He's lying in a hospital bed, hooked up with painkillers, trying to deal with his own reality. You have been working on this case for 30 years and all you can do is laugh?"

Quinlan swallowed hard. All eyes in the restaurant were on them. He tried to reach for her to sit down. Chrissy pulled away. "No, I'm leaving now. You can keep your evidence. Maybe you can even find a killer if that's not too much to ask. I'm going to take a real shower in a real house and lie in a real bed because I'm .... real .... tired."

He watched her bulldoze her way past the crowded restaurant. Quinlan carefully put the jewelry back in the pouch and looked at one piece that still had the sales tag attached. It read: Tiffany $14,000.

"I'll be damned."

The bicycle was stuck in the mud ... lightning flashed ... he couldn't move ... faces came from every direction... bloodied...mouths open in silent screams .... Abe ... Frances ... Max ...

"No!" Buddy screamed. He sat upright in his bed with his eyes wild with fright. He was still dreaming, still hallucinating from the drugs they gave him for pain. "Help me. Help me ... mmph ..." A hand covered his mouth. It was a calloused hand, not a hospital hand, and the face was the old man that Buddy met at the flea mart. Buddy struggled to talk but couldn't break the grip.

"Shhhh. You were dreamin', son. Don't yell out. I'm here to help you. Okay?"

Buddy shook his head up and down. The old man released his grip. "You're — you're the old man from the flea mart. The one that sold me the box of movies."

"That's right."

"Who are you? How did you get those movies?"

"Those are mine. Took 'em myself." He peered over wireless glasses into Buddy's eyes.

Buddy felt the blood rush out of his head. He looked into those eyes and saw it right away. There was no mistaking it. "Oh my God. It's you, isn't it?"

Abe looked over his shoulder and saw the guard coming back down the hall from the men's room. "I don't have much time, son."

He looked at Buddy and lost his train of thought. "You are so grown up, son. There have been many things that I have done in the past that I regret," Abe's voice cracked with each word. "Your mother ... Buddy ... I ..."

Footsteps grew louder at the door. Abe ducked down next to the bed as Officer Sambito stepped in. "Everything alright in here, Buddy?"

Buddy grabbed his shoulder and grimaced in pain. "That pain in my shoulder is back. Could you just let the nurses know?"

"Sure thing. I'll be right back."

Abe popped up quickly. He pulled out a slip of paper from his coat pocket. "Tell Chrissy to come to this address tomorrow night at 8. She's family. I can trust her. I've got a package that tells it all. Don't tell anyone else, okay?"

Buddy lay frozen. He wanted to say so many things to his dad that were buried for years. They both just looked at each other. Abe held his hand. "You ... better get out of here," Buddy finally said as he heard Sambito's voice in the distance.

Abe shuffled to the door and peeked out. He looked back at Buddy and said, "See ya, slugger." He opened the door quickly and walked down the hall as Sambito turned the corner.

Buddy watched him through the doorway until he disappeared.

"Did you see that old guy?" Sambito asked as he entered Buddy's room.

"What old guy?"

"Some old guy passed me. He was crying pretty hard. Must've lost someone who was close to him." Sambito ducked into the bathroom.

"Maybe." Tears started to stream down his cheeks. "— or maybe he just found someone close to him," Buddy said to himself as looked down the long corridor.

He wiped his eyes.

The phone was ringing as soon as Chrissy opened the door. Balancing her keys and two bags of groceries, she stumbled to the phone knocking the receiver over on the floor.

"I'll be right there — sorry, whoever you are. "Chrissy screamed to the receiver. She dropped all the groceries on the kitchen counter and scooped up the phone. "Hello?"

"Dancing again are we, darlin'?" The raspy voice on the other end was familiar, though weak and strained.

"Daddy, I'm just practicing for you."

"Well, by the sound of it, you need to keep practicing."

"I was just coming to see you. I'm putting the groceries away and I'll be right..."

"No, honey. It's late. I don't want you coming all the way over here. I'll be asleep anyway." Buddy had a hard time getting out the last few words. His lungs were wheezing. He felt that every part of his body was wheezing.

"You don't want me to come by?" Chrissy sat down slowly on the floor.

"Sure, I do. First thing tomorrow. I've got something very important to tell you, but I don't want to tell you on the phone."

"Me too. I had a conversation with that detective and he told me all kinds of things about the family."

"Don't tell me tonight. Tell me in the morning. Please, honey, it's important that we talk in person." Buddy hoped she understood. He felt even more paranoia after speaking to his dad. What if the phones were bugged? He prayed silently that Chrissy would be safe.

"Okay, you old crank. I'll be there first thing in the morning." Chrissy actually felt a sigh of relief. She could finally get some rest. "Can I bring you anything?"

"There's that 'Playboy' on my dresser that I wanted to read."

"Oh, stop. You don't have the strength to turn the pages much less look at the ..."

"... articles? Yes, the articles. That's why I buy the darn thing."

"You are impossible."

"Hey, speaking of impossible, have you called your mother?"

"Not yet."

"Do it. She's probably worried. You know I didn't have a chance to ask, 'How is your Mom?' " The last line they said together and laughed.

"The plastic surgeon skipped out," Chrissy ad libbed to make it interesting. "She was very depressed."

"Clinically or economically?"

"Anatomically."

"Anatomically?"

"Yeah. He lifted her up and let her down."

Buddy burst into laughter. He also almost burst his lung again as he sputtered out his last laugh. "Hey, you're good."

"I've been practicing that one for weeks."

"You've got a career in standup my dear. Actually it's a good thing. Your dance career ended abruptly tonight."

"Crank."

"Flatterer."

"Go to sleep. Kisses."

"Back at ya. Love you darlin'."

"Love you too, daddy. Good night."

Chrissy hung up the phone and turned toward the kitchen. It was only then that she looked at the apartment. Really looked. It was trashed. Chairs overturned, couches turned inside out, papers on the floor, boxes overturned.

She did a 360 just like a captain in a submarine periscope. It made her dizzy. She staggered to the nearest cushionless chair, found the missing seat and plopped down with her face in her hands.

"Oh, my God," said the voice coming from behind her. It was Andi. She looked down at Chrissy from the open doorway. "Oh, sweetie, I can't believe this."

Chrissy just looked up and managed a weak smile. "Hi, Andi. Welcome to paradise."

"Are you okay? Were you hurt? Can I get you something?" Andi continued to babble as she started to pick up what was on the floor.

"Don't touch anything!" Chrissy suddenly screamed.

Andi jumped back. "Oh!"

"I'm so sorry. I didn't mean to scream at you. It's just that I bet the cops will want to check for clues, you know?"

"Of course, honey. How stupid of me." Andi started to put the things she moved back where she found them.

"Just sit with me for a while, Andi, until the cops come." Chrissy shook her head. "I guess it would be helpful if I actually called them, huh?"

Andi managed a short laugh. "Would you like me to call them?"

"No thanks. But you could hand me the phone, if you don't mind."

"Sure." Andi picked up the receiver and handed it to Chrissy. She dug into her bag and fished out Quinlan's card from the pocket of her knapsack purse. No matter how much junk Chrissy carried, she always seemed to find what she was looking for.

She dialed the direct number to Quinlan's cell phone. The deep hoarse voice answered. "Quinlan."

"Hi, it's Chrissy. I, um, just had visitors."

"Are they still there?"

"No. They left before I came home. But they certainly didn't have good manners."

"I'll be right over."

Chrissy hung up. "I can't wait."

Andi looked over at her. "Quinlan's not on your top 10 list, is he?"

"Oh, he's okay, I guess. I'm just not used to cops. They are so, I don't know, abrupt. At least that's how Quinlan is. Doesn't seem to like women very much."

"Maybe he wasn't ever married."

"Or had a mother."

"I bet he was raised by wolves." Chrissy made the face that Quinlan makes when he snarls and curls his lip. Andi laughed and hugged Chrissy.

"Speaking of raised by wolves, is your father, the big bad wolf, recovering nicely?"

"Yeah, seems to be. I talked to him tonight. He wanted me to come by in the morning. He seemed pretty adamant about tomorrow, said he had some things to tell me."

"He's not thinking he's dying. Is he?"

"No, I don't think so. The doctor told me this afternoon that he should make a full recovery. I think there's something else he wants to tell me."

"You know Chrissy, he loves you very much." Andi pushed Chrissy's hair off her forehead like she was a little child. Andi never had children. She wanted to be a mother ever since she could remember.

Chrissy straightened up, "Have you guys been together long?"

"About a year now."

"You're not sick of him yet?"

"Sure, I'm sick of him, but he's the last single guy I know who's straight."

The pain of that last comment stabbed her in the chest. Images of Stan and his boyfriend popped up in her head. She managed a smile. "You mean he told you he was straight?"

Andi laughed again. This time it was a hearty laugh. Chrissy was drawn to her. Something about her eyes made you feel that she had been through pain. Even that hearty laugh couldn't hide the sadness in her face.

"Chrissy, your dad is a wonderful man. I know you know that."

"He's okay."

"This last year has been so special to me. I was alone an awfully long time. I was raised by a couple that didn't really love me. I never knew my mom and my dad abandoned me when I was very young. They took me in. They tried ... but I never got over losing my real Dad."

"Do you ever see your real dad?"

"No ... he died a while ago."

Chrissy looked at Andi. "I think that's what scares the most ... this is the first time I ever really thought about Dad not being there, you know? I think of him as never ... dying."

"He's not going anywhere; he'll be safe. We will both take good care of him."

Chrissy looked at her watch. "Oh, I almost forgot. I need to call my mother."

"Okay, I'll make a deal with you. You call your mom and I'll powder my whatever; that is if the toilet hasn't been stolen."

Andi spent a longer than usual time in the bathroom so that Chrissy could have some privacy. When she came out, Chrissy was looking through photos of Buddy and Andi.

"Hope you don't mind, Andi, these were in the only box that seemed to be untouched."

"Well, he was probably scared by the faces."

"You two go a lot of places. Hey, look at this one," Chrissy pulled out a picture of Buddy posed holding an old Palms Motel sign. "This was where the old Palms once was."

"I know."

"Did you take that one?"

"Yes. We went there a couple of months ago. It was a strange feeling."

"Did you know about the Palms before?"

"You know, I stayed there as a kid."

"How ironic. Did Daddy and you ever know each other then?"

"Not really."

Suddenly the door opened. The hulking figure of Quinlan filled the doorway. Looking around he saw the two figures of Chrissy and Andi, both looking like school girls with photo albums, seated on the floor.

Chrissy pushed the elevator button for the second floor. The elevator had a strong smell of disinfectant mixed with urine, the unmistakable hospital odor that makes you want to be anywhere but there. Chrissy silently prayed that the doors would open soon. No matter how much they renovate hospitals, Chrissy thought, they still have that godawful smell.

The doors opened to a new odor. Chrissy couldn't place it at first but as she walked down the hallway and saw the open rooms filled with old faces, she realized it was the smell of death. That's what she always thought about when she was around older people. She put her head down and walked a little faster.

She almost ran headfirst into Officer Sambito, who had turned to face her as she scurried to the room.

"Excuse me ma'am," Sambito caught her arm, "I'll have to see some ID before I let you in."

"Hmm?"

"Identification please, ma'am."

"Oh, yes. Let's see," Chrissy rummaged through her knapsack and found her license. "Here it is."

Sambito checked his clipboard. "Okay, Ms. Rosen. Thank you." He opened the door for her.

Chrissy walked to Buddy's bed. He was breathing heavily with a wheezing sound. His mouth was open and he was hooked up to IVs hanging from the bedside poles. One shoulder of his hospital gown was opened and Chrissy could see the heavily bandaged chest that was the entry point of the .44 Magnum bullet that pierced his lung and just missed his heart.

Buddy cried in his sleep.

"Oh, Daddy. You must be in so much pain." Chrissy held his hand. "It's okay. It's okay."

"Chrissy?" Buddy looked at her eyes. "Have you been here long?"

"Not too long." Chrissy placed his hand next to her face and kissed it.

"I'm glad you came, honey. Have you been alright?"

"I'm fine." Chrissy fixed his pillow and lifted his head slightly. "Andi came by last night and told me to tell you that she's thinking about you. She's going to visit after work."

"Good."

"Daddy, someone broke in last night."

Buddy raised his eyebrows, "What? Were you there?"

"No, it happened before I got home. Detective Quinlan came over and I spent the night with Andi at her place."

"What was missing?"

"Don't know. We just left stuff where it was left so the police could get evidence."

"The movies?"

"I think Detective Quinlan has them."

"You gave them to him?"

"He got them from your car after you were shot. He knows a lot about the family. A lot about Abe and Frances. He said that Abe and Frances are dead. The films were fakes."

"No, Chrissy ... listen," Buddy motioned for her to lean down so that he could whisper in her ear. "Abe came to visit me."

"You were probably dreaming."

"No. He was here. He was also the flea mart salesman that sold me the films. He came into my room yesterday — sat right here and told me how he escaped death."

"Daddy, he's dead."

"No, honey. When I saw him at the flea mart he wanted to tell me then, but he was being watched."

"Let's say he is alive and he did come to see you and got past Barney Fife outside. What did he want you to do?"

"He didn't have time to tell me. There's something he has for me and he wants to give it to you."

"Me?"

"Yes, honey. This evening at 8:00 PM at the entrance to Hubbard's Pier he wants you to meet him. He's scared, Chrissy."

"But — shouldn't the police."

"No police. He doesn't trust anyone."

"Okay. I'll meet him." Chrissy hugged Buddy and he held her tightly. He handed her the note that Abe gave to him.

"There's something else I want you to do for me."

"Oh, great. This isn't enough?"

"Look in the top drawer of the carrier by the wall."

Chrissy obliged. She pulled out a stack of papers. The sheet on top was headed: To The Most Wonderful Class I Had This Week.

"Take these to my classroom today, please, and read the top sheet to them."

"Just like it is?"

"Just like it is."

"Anything else?"

"Nope."

"Am I dismissed?"

"Aye, Captain."

"I love you, Rosen." She kissed him on top of the head.

"You ain't so bad yourself, Rosen."

Each classroom of Coquina Prep faced the courtyard. It was easy to spot kids, because of the glass doors. This provided a mixed blessing for teachers. On the one hand, there was an open feeling of space. On the other hand, that same space was a huge distraction for some of the kids.

When Chrissy walked through the courtyard, two classes were playing volleyball. She spotted one of the teachers, who watched nearby.

Chrissy scooted past an errant foul ball, "Excuse me, do you know where Buddy Rosen's classroom is?"

Becky Sue Wright raised her eyebrows in a questioning pose," Mr. Rosen is not here on campus anymore."

Anymore? Chrissy wondered why she chose those words. "I just wanted to visit his classroom for a couple of minutes."

"Are you a parent?"

"No —." Chrissy was about to introduce herself but was interrupted.

"You need to check in at the office. That is our policy. They will point you in the right direction."

"Thank you, Miss ... ?" Chrissy extended her hand.

Becky shook her hand by the fingers. "That's, Mrs. Becky Sue Wright."

"Nice to meet you." Chrissy started to introduce herself again but thought better of it.

"Chrissy?" Across the courtyard came a familiar voice. Andi ran up to her. "This is a nice surprise. What are you doing here?"

"Hi ... I came to visit Daddy's classroom to give them something he had written for them." Becky Sue was within earshot and leaned in to hear the rest.

"Come with me," Andi continued. "I'll show you where it is."

"Should I check in at the office?"

"Not unless you're an axe murderer."

Becky Sue gave a haughty tilt of her head. She turned and walked to the other side of the courtyard toward a group of teachers sitting on benches under the trees.

Chrissy watched her leave and asked Andi, "What's the story with Mrs. Becky Sue Wright?"

"She's the unofficial news source for the entire campus, our very own of 'National Enquirer.' Did you have the pleasure of meeting her?"

"Oh, yes."

"Then you can count on your life story being recounted as we speak." Andi nodded in her direction. By this time, Becky Sue had approached the group and looked like an orchestra conductor waving her arms in an animated discussion. Every few seconds she would tilt her head in the direction of Andi and Chrissy. "Your dad went for her throat every chance he got."

"I bet he did."

"That's your dad's class, eating lunch." Andi motioned to the far corner of the courtyard. "Are you hungry?"

"Sure."

"Then you're not ready for school food. It's better if you've already eaten and only want to pass through."

"I'll chance it."

"I see you have inherited your father's sense of adventure. Follow me."

Chrissy and Andi headed to the cafeteria. "We must be getting close," Chrissy said. "I can hear the sounds of silverware and trays falling to the floor."

"You have good instincts." Andi motioned around the corner. "Here's our first stop."

The cafeteria was just what she expected. Lines of kids playfully pushing and talking loudly as teams of teachers shuffled through to herd the masses like well trained sheep dogs keeping the stragglers in line.

There was one area for drinks and desserts. This seemed to be for those children who brought a bag lunch and just wanted extras. There were a few lines dedicated to hot lunch and an area for prepackaged sandwiches. Chrissy was actually very impressed. What seemed like mass chaos at first was really more like controlled chaos.

"What's your poison?" Andi asked. "This line has dry grilled cheese sandwiches and wet potato chips. Over here we have the stew of a thousand beans and char broiled hot dogs and finally there seems to be a fruit medley that was left here last week."

"Mmmm — choices are extensive. I'll brave the medley."

"Okay. Check your weapons." Andi and Chrissy braved their way through the crowd and picked up two fruit bowls lined up under the sneeze guards. They made their way outside to an empty picnic table.

"Chrissy, you earned your first stripes in action."

"Wasn't painful at all." Chrissy laughed as she placed her food down in front of her.

"Excuse me, ladies. Are these seats taken?" Bob Kevin bowed next to the picnic table as if he was in the presence of royalty.

"Be our guest, Mr. Kevin." Andi said as she motioned to a place next to her.

"Chrissy, this is Bob Kevin, fourth grade teacher and best friend of your dad." Chrissy held out her hand.

Bob placed his tray down and took her hand in both of his. "No need to introduce yourself, Chrissy, I know all about you. Becky Sue Wright filled me in." He nodded in her general direction.

"Well then, I'm sure you know everything that you need to know," Chrissy giggled as she looked over her shoulder in

Becky Sue's direction. Becky Sue turned her head away quickly as Chrissy looked at her.

"So, how is that slacker father of yours? Is it true what Becky Sue says, that he really wasn't shot? He's just looking for an excuse to get out of class?"

"Of course that's not true," Chrissy winked. "He's drying out in an alcohol rehab hospital. Becky Sue should have known that."

"Buddy's kid," Kevin said. "How is he really doing?"

"He's hanging in there. The doctors say that he should be fully recovered in time. It's his lungs I worry about."

"Well, he never was a great singer. So I think we're safe there." Kevin looked at Andi.

"He misses you all. There have been lots of cards from his kids and well-wishers. I know that he thinks about you guys all the time."

"It's only 'cause he owes me 50 bucks. I told him that the interest didn't start for a few months."

Chrissy shook her head and smiled again. "Andi, you hang with these guys?"

"Only when I'm desperate for an abusive relationship. I try to lie down and wait for that feeling to pass."

"Art teachers are always desperate," Bob took a quick bite of his cold cheese sandwich then stood up. "And I am desperate for a Tums. Ladies, it's been a true pleasure."

"Same here," Chrissy said.

"Desperation becomes you," Andi said.

"Tell your dad I'm thinking of him. I'll send him a copy of 'Becky Sue's Greatest Hits,' recorded live on the playground. It's kind of a cheering up thing."

“I’ll be sure to let him know. I’m sure he’ll return the favor.”

“Are you ladies up for refreshments after school?” He looked at Chrissy. “This is how teachers make it through the night and get the courage to come back in the morning.”

“I sure you could use one,” Chrissy said.

Andi answered, “Sorry Chrissy, I’m turning in early. Kevin ... Take good care of this girl.”

“Okay — if that’s the way you wanna be. Oops, Principal Rankin headed our way. Really gotta split now. Adios, Chrissy, I’ll meet you at Manny’s at 7.” Kevin slipped around the table and out of sight.

Miss Rankin approached. “You must be Buddy’s daughter.”

“Why yes, I’m Chrissy.” Chrissy extended her hand.

“Very nice to meet you. I am Miss Rankin, principal of Coquina. I hope your dad is progressing well?”

“Yes, ma’am. He is doing fine. I will tell him that you were asking about him.”

“Please do. If there is anything I can do, don’t hesitate to call.”

“Thank you.” Chrissy stood and shook her hand again. She was at least 3 inches taller than Miss Rankin.

“Good day.”

Andi whispered as Miss Rankin headed toward the cafeteria. “She’s a tough old bird, but I think she really likes your dad despite his constant teasing and unconventional teaching methods.”

“Hard not to like him, huh?” Chrissy asked.

“Very. Now, let’s dump the fruit and get to class.”

"Students ... students. Can I have your attention?"

Mrs. Skidmore, the thin, wiry substitute teacher that was in charge of Buddy's class, hit the desk lightly to accent her words. She looked as if to be in her late 50's or early 60's, greying temples and black wispy hair falling around her shoulders. Glasses framed her angular features, which were covered in heavy makeup. Pencil thin eyebrow liner drawn on delicately covered a lack of real eyebrows.

"I wanted to introduce you to a visitor. This is Miss Chrissy Rosen. She is the daughter of Mr. Rosen and she has something that she's brought for us.

"Miss Rosen?"

Chrissy was standing by the chalkboard and walked up to the front of the classroom as Mrs. Skidmore introduced her. She smiled at the students as their eyes studied her carefully. She carried the stack of papers under her arm.

"Hi." Chrissy put the papers on the desk and picked up the one on top. "My dad says hello and wanted me to tell you that he was doing fine. He hopes to be back real soon."

A hand shot up in the back of the room.

"You have a question?" Chrissy craned her neck slightly to see Robert Dowling's face.

Robert stood and cleared his throat. "What does Mr. Rosen want to do about Shithead?"

Chrissy looked at Mrs. Skidmore, "Did he just say ..."

"I'll explain later," Mrs Skidmore said. "Robert, we've already put a feeding schedule together for the snake. Let's move on."

"Okay, well, here goes. My dad wrote a poem for you guys and he asked me to read it. So listen up:

"To The Best Class I Ever Had ... Today
I miss your faces, I miss your smiles,
The tribulations and the trials,
Billy Moore and Billy Gross
Do you still believe in ghosts?
Hillary and Steven, too
Please don't fight till I get through
Stacey Barnes keep up your math
Thomas Foley stay the path
Read the pledge Josh Ferguson
Write your play Fred Washington
Robert feed the snake each day
His name is Voltaire, by the way
Remember, always, it's the rule
To share your kindness while in school
Me mines are the enemies
Friends of ours are thanks and please.
When I come back, I'll give you hugs
Now work real hard and don't be slugs."

"What's tripolashuns?"

"I bet you are Joshua Ferguson," Chrissy said as she looked down the paper at a note that her dad had scribbled in the margins: Joshua Ferguson will probably ask what "tribulation" means.

"Uh-huh," Joshua Ferguson said.

"It means something that is difficult, a thing that is really hard for you to do."

"Like pullups?" asked Billy Gross.

"No, silly, like war or something," Hillary piped in.

"Actually, you are both right." Chrissy said. "Tribulations are a bunch of things that cause difficulty."

"Is Mr. Rosen gonna get better?" Valerie Saron asked.

Chrissy couldn't help herself as a tear slowly trailed down her cheek. She looked at those beautiful faces and saw what her dad saw. She understood the love he felt for these students and for a few precious seconds, struggled with her answer. "Yes ... yes, he is. And he really misses you guys. He gets all your cards and he thinks of you all the time. He wrote something special to everybody. I'm gonna leave these with your teacher." Chrissy handed the stack of paper to Mrs. Skidmore. "Is there anything you'd like me to tell Mr. Rosen or give him for you?"

Thomas Foley stood up and walked toward Chrissy. He handed her a wrinkled brown lunch bag. Chrissy looked down and said, "Would you like me to give this to Mr. Rosen?"

"It's a peanut butter sandwich. I've been savin' it for him."

The storm hit at about 6:45 in the evening. Sheets of rain pelted Chrissy's car as she tried to maneuver the slick streets of St. Pete. Stoplights blinked yellow at some intersections, others were just dark. That old feeling of dread crept over her as she pulled into a parking spot in front of Manny's Bar. This was where her dad was shot. Bob Kevin waited inside. Maybe somebody else remembers something.

"Well," she thought, "I have a half hour to kill (bad choice of words) before I go to Hubbard's Pier to meet Dad's nightmare, if he really exists."

Chrissy shook out her hair as she stepped in the bar. She spotted Kevin at a table that was in a corner. She made a beeline to the far chair.

"Hey there little Rosen," Kevin said, "had to swim here, huh?"

"Just about. Is this your usual table?"

"Nope. Your dad and I sit up there most times." Kevin said pointing to the bar. "I just figured there were less tattoos over here and you might be more comfortable."

Chrissy pulled her hair back and leaned in front of Kevin so he could see her neck. There was a tiny red heart tattooed in the middle of her neck right on the hairline.

"Wow ... look at you ... a regular Hell's Angel. Guess you'd feel comfortable with more of your kind like Squeaky and Tiny up there." Squeaky and Tiny were two bikers that were painted head-to-toe under their leather jackets and bandanas. Tiny was about 300 pounds and Squeaky had a baritone voice (and a pet mouse).

Chrissy laughed.

"So what's the story behind the baby heart?"

Chrissy brushed her hair back again. "It was my one rebellious move against my mother. She and I were fighting — again — and I had a friend that asked me if I wanted to go with her to get this done and I ... did it."

"What did your mom say?"

"She still doesn't know."

“Seems like a waste of rebellious in-your-face messaging if you ask me.”

“Well, it was just the fact that I did it and have kept it my little secret that’s important.”

“Any significance to the heart?”

“Nope. Just the smallest thing I could think of.”

“You … rebel!”

Debbie came over to the table. “Would you like your umbrella drink served over here tonight, Kevin?”

“Maybe … Debbie. I’d like you to meet Miss Christina Rosen.” Debbie stood in front of Chrissy with one hand on her hip and the other holding a bar towel at her side. She looked her square in the face. “That’s where I’ve seen that face. Buddy shows us your picture all the time. You’re Christina.”

“Yes. I’m Christina.”

“Manny, come over here,” Debbie yelled across the bar to Manny, who was serving a beer to Jake the Plumber. “It’s Buddy’s kid, Christina. Look.”

Chrissy tried to make herself look small as all heads in the bar turned in her direction, but she managed to smile weakly and wave.

“No shit. Really?” Manny yelled back. “Hey, girl. Don’t go anywhere, I’ll be right over.”

Debbie put a big meaty arm around Christina’s shoulders and sat down next to her. “How is he? We’ve been thinking, about him you know?”

“He’s hanging in there… still really weak, but he’s going to be all right.”

“Good, good.” Manny came up behind Chrissy as she finished her last words. He sat two beers down … one in front of her and one for Kevin … and pulled up the chair next to her on the opposite side that Debbie sat. "That old shit. Nobody's gonna keep him down."

Chrissy looked at the beer, then up at Debbie. She winked and nodded. "Go ahead, honey," Debbie said." It's on the house."

"Thanks," Chrissy answered. She took a sip. "He was shot right outside of here, wasn't he?"

Debbie and Manny looked at each other and at Kevin. Finally, Manny spoke. "That's right. I was the first one to find him. I ran outside when I heard the shot," Manny said as he made the gesture of a handgun with his fingers.

"You heard the gunshot in here?"

"Well, actually, I heard it from the kitchen." He pointed to the door next to the bar. "I ran out the back door to the alley. He was lying right next to his car."

"Was he conscious?" Chrissy asked as she took another sip.

"He was drifting in and out. There was so much blood. He was choking on it."

"Manny!" Debbie interrupted. She raised her eyebrows. "You don't have to go into every detail in front of Christina. It's her daddy, remember."

"That's okay, really." Chrissy touched his arm. "The police told me all about it. Besides, I'm the one who asked the question." Chrissy finished off the rest of her beer, feeling much more relaxed now. "Thank you for being there for him. I know how close you both are to Daddy."

"He's our favorite barfly," Debbie said as they all laughed.

"Do the cops have any idea who it was?" Manny asked.

"Not really."

"I've been telling him for years to sell this damn bar," Debbie said looking around the room. "I said, 'Manny, why don't we just get out of this neighborhood, maybe get a place on the north side of town?' I don't feel safe when I'm here by myself and I have to lock up — even though we keep a big ol' magnum pistol behind the bar."

There was a crash at the bar. Chrissy nearly jumped out of her skin. "It's only Jake," Manny said to Chrissy as he patted her shoulder. "He falls off the stool once or twice a night. I better go help him up. You want another beer?"

"Oh, no thanks. I have to get going." Chrissy stood. "I'm glad I had the chance to meet you both. Thank you for everything."

"Don't mention it, honey. We're here if you need us." Debbie hugged her.

"That's right, you just let us know. Tell the ol' shit we were thinking of him," Manny said as he hugged Chrissy too.

Christina walked toward the door just when Billy wheeled his bicycle past the jukebox and threw it down in front of the bar.

"Hey, Manny, where are them receipts?"

Bernie was dying.

As he sat in the dark on a lonely bench, he thought about parts of his body falling off one by one. His liver was shot, then his stomach would probably go, kidneys — aw, hell — who was he kidding? The liver was going to kill him way before any of that. The doctor gave him a "short time." He had to push him for that answer. "I don't know why doctors don't want to tell you the truth," he muttered under his breath. I'm dying. I know it — you know it — just tell me how long.

A short time.

He didn't tell Wayne, but Wayne knew. He just never talked about it. He was happy to have that old fart as his friend.

He looked through the package that he made for Chrissy. In it was everything she needed to protect her father and to protect herself. The SOBs ... yeah ... they sure were. Slimy old Jimmy Bennett. Hah. Senator James Bennett. As crooked as they come. He and his little weasel assistant Phillips really did a number on him.

He knew the first time Bennett gave him a stack of hundreds — the first step to making The Palms a destination for his cronies — he was selling his soul to the devil. They came from everywhere. He handpicked them: attorneys, accountants, contractors; he even suckered Oscar Martinez, the squeaky clean protector of the beaches to be his shield. He built the Save Our Beaches Foundation as the front door to protect all his dirty money.

Oscar never knew.

The Foundation grew and the mission to protect the beaches ironically flourished. Until the day he died, Oscar Martinez thought that his Foundation was beyond reproach. He became an important man. He never questioned how all the money appeared in the coffers. Bennett and Phillips took care of that. "Government grants and wealthy donors," Oscar thought.

Abe Rosen knew differently.

He was on the "inside." Bennett trusted him. Abe was an SOB. The secret meetings, the fancy rings, the special favors

— Abe enjoyed them. But Abe talked too much at times — especially when he was drunk. Frances asked too many questions and Abe became abusive.

She was not comfortable with what was happening at their "beach paradise."

Abe thought: "She would have been more than unhappy if she knew the rest of the story."

Bennett owned Insurance Agencies around the state. He knew how to work the system. One of the prerequisites for membership in the SOB was buying a low cost insurance policy naming the Save Our Beaches Foundation as beneficiary. Initially, the plan was as the members aged and passed, there would be a steady income stream filling the coffers of the Foundation.

Membership grew — but the members didn't age fast enough.

Bennett and Phillips came up with a new plan. The Barody Brothers fit the bill nicely. Every couple of months, Abe heard about a construction accident that took the life of an SOB who lived in Ohio; or a car accident victim in Michigan; a heart attack in Alabama. These were friends — people who Abe grew fond of — he was over it. He wanted to cut ties, but didn't know how.

He bought a storage unit and squirreled away things that he could use in case he had to get away. He thought of it as his fallout shelter — when he fell out of sight from those who would be looking for him. He put boxes of clothing, supplies, evidence that would incriminate the SOB inner circle — even his precious home movies. There were supplies for everyone: him, Frannie and Buddy.

Abe thought back to the night he woke up in the boat — head spinning — Frannie lying dead on the floor. He pulled Frannie overboard with him and swam to shore in the dead of night. He buried her beneath the heavy underbrush.

There was nothing left for him. Selma would take care of Buddy — better than he would — he had left the Palms to Buddy in his will and had put a copy in the safety deposit box. One day he would return and it would be there.

He read about Ralph hanging himself in jail. Time passed and Abe watched Buddy grow from afar. It got harder to come back.

He heard a sound. Bernie stuffed the documents and a couple of films in a big envelope and put it under the bench.

It was pitch black ... he could hardly see his hand in front of his eyes. "Who's there? Chrissy? Is that you?"

Flashes of lighting lit up the sky as Chrissy made her way to the beach.

The warm feeling she had after drinking a beer at Manny's gave way to a cold shudder at the thought of coming face-to-face with her grandfather. "He's not a nice man" kept replaying around in her head. Maybe he had changed. After all, look at the chances he took to meet her and to help daddy, she thought.

Every so often, Chrissy glanced in her rearview mirror for police cars or "bad guys" who might be tailing her. She crossed the familiar bridge to John's Pass and looked at the large seafood restaurant signs that she remembered from her childhood. The comfortable stilt buildings and the long pier still stood as a reminder of days past, even though they had been remodeled and in some cases, totally rebuilt.

When she reached the pier she slowed down to once again check her mirror and look around for any signs of unwelcome guests. She decided to park at the end of the pier and walk along with the crowd. She broke from the crowd only when she felt quite certain that she was alone and quickly crossed to the boat slips.

Slip 19 was easy to spot. There was a large wooden houseboat tied to the supports. It looked as if it were at least 30 years old , but was in pretty good condition. There was a light on inside that peeked from under the shutters and danced up and down with the rocking rhythm of the gulf.

There was a wooden bench under a burned-out streetlight that faced the slip. Christina walked back and forth for a few minutes, looking in every direction for any sign of her grandfather. She couldn't remember if her dad had said to meet at slip 19 or to meet on the boat in slip 19. She glanced at her watch. It was 8:13 PM. She stepped back toward the bench and felt an object beneath her foot. She bent down to see what it was: It was an envelope with her name on it. Slowly, she put it inside her backpack and bent to sit on the darkened bench.

Christina felt a little more comfortable back in the shadows, where she could see everything but couldn't be seen herself. She glanced over her shoulder and caught her breath. There was a figure of a man or something sitting right next to her. She strained to look a little closer. "Hello? Grandfather, is that you?"

There was no answer.

Christina stood and started to move back into the light, and put her backpack on. When she looked down she saw that her strap was covered with blood and so was her hand. She looked at her shirt and jeans. They were wet with blood. The bench was covered with blood as well. Pure fear gripped her. She backed up and turned to run. There was a dark figure in her path and she flew right into his arms.

Christina cried out and tried to run, but the dark figure had her in his grasp.

"Well, well, well. What are you doing here, Ms. Rosen?" said the voice from the shadows.

"Are you gonna kill me too?" Christina's voice was shaky but remained strong.

"Only if you continue to mess up my investigation. Babysitting you has become a way of life," said Quinlan as he released the grip.

Christina breathed a sigh of relief. "Oh, man, It's you. I thought you were the murderer."

"Murderer of who?" Quinlan asked.

"Him!" Christina pointed to the figure.

Quinlan walked to the figure and touched his shoulder. The figure fell headfirst from the bench and then flopped on his back in the light. His eyes were wide open and his throat was cut from one end to the other.

"My God," Chrissy turned away. "Is it —?"

"It's Abe. I'll be goddamned, it's Abe."

"Is he dead?" Chrissy asked.

Quinlan knelt next to Abe's head and felt for any sign of life. "Been dead for over an hour by the looks of it." Quinlan suddenly stood up and walked toward Chrissy. "Chrissy how the hell did you wind up here? How did you know —"

He was interrupted by a familiar loud ringing sound. He fumbled around his coat pocket and pulled out his cell phone. "Yeah! It's Quinlan. What? No shit! Where's Sambito? I'm heading to the hospital right now. Call headquarters will ya? Dead body at slip 19 St. Pete Beach." He jammed his phone back into his pocket and turned to Christina, "Come on. You drive with me. It's easier than following you."

"What are we doing?"

He looked her squarely in the eyes, "We're keeping your father alive."

Sambito's eyes got heavy as he sat against the wall in front of Buddy's room. He had one cup of coffee at 4 but needed a refresher. It was one of those late afternoon siestas that come up unexpectedly, he thought, as he wrestled over in his mind how he could take a break before he broke his neck when his head fell over. He called security on his mobile. "Tyrone, Sambito here; hey, listen, my friend, can you do me a great favor and cover for me for a few while I go for coffee? Five minutes ... that would be fine thanks."

"So, we're getting a little sleepy, are we?" Sambito turned to see Evelyn Moorehouse, a late-shift nurse on three south who was leaning on the wall behind him.

"Yeah, Ev, I guess these old eyes aren't what they used to be."

"And just what was it they used to be, Joe?"

"Better, I guess."

Evelyn looked down at him with her lids half closed, "They still look good to me."

Joe turned red and looked away for a second. "Thanks, Evelyn. I suppose if I can't get them to work good, they can at least look good."

"You know, I can make a mean carrot cake, or fix you up with some cool ... sliced ... raw carrots too, Joe. Anytime you want to test your eyesight you just give Evelyn a call, okay?"

Joe's face felt hot and crimson as he stammered, "I'll do that, Ev." Since his divorce a year ago, Joe had met with some interesting propositions and was uncomfortable with all of them. Evelyn had latched onto him as soon as she saw that he wasn't wearing a ring. She was a veteran divorcée. Fifteen years on her own, Evelyn raised three kids single handedly and now as a grandmother of two, she no longer stood on ceremony. She knew what she wanted and she went for it.

Tyrone Covington walked up to Joe just as he was about to run out of all the "aw shucks, ma'am" comments he could muster. "Tyrone, thanks for taking a shift."

Joe said it in such a desperate voice that Tyrone took a step back. "Well, you don't have to slobber all over me, Sambito. It ain't like I was buying you flowers or something."

Evelyn laughed and waved to Joe as she turned to walk down the hall. "Mmmm she loves you."

"Just shut up. I'll be back in a five minutes." Sambito barked as he headed to the elevators.

Tyrone called to him, "Now that's more like the Joe I know."

Joe didn't pay any attention to Tyrone, nor did he notice the person who stepped into the elevator behind him right before the doors closed.

Max was laughing loudly, hysterically...
Pedals grew large on his bicycle...
The lightning flashed and thunder clapped ...

Buddy sat up, drenched with sweat as the lightning flashed and a clap of thunder crashed again outside. His breathing was labored and his chest burned from the pain. He groaned and lay down on the pillow. He wanted to cry out, but all he could muster was a whimper.

Tyrone Covington heard the movement through the cracked doorway and peeked in as Buddy lay back down. He looked at his watch. "Man, where is that Sambito? He's been gone for over an hour." Tyrone wandered over to the nurse's station to tell them about Buddy's dream.

Buddy drifted back to sleep. The wheezing was much lighter than it had been when he was first admitted, but the pain in his chest had remained. Every few minutes, Buddy would wince as he took a deep breath.

His visitor quietly walked into the room and sat in the light blue chair that faced the hospital bed. Buddy's room was filled with fresh flowers from Andi and get-well cards that stood on the window sill like protective soldiers. Overhead were new drawings sent by his students. One was a picture of Buddy in bed with a great big smile that flew off his face. There was also a nurse, who looked to be twice his size, holding a shot that could have killed a horse. The caption read: "Git Well Soon, Mr. Rosen. Take Yur Medusin! Love, Josh."

The visitor smiled at the pictures and adjusted the blue chair. It creaked slightly as it was moved to the head of the bed.

"How much longer?" Chrissy asked as the car shifted into the left lane.

"A few minutes," Quinlan said. "If we don't get stuck in traffic again." Quinlan looked up ahead and saw the lines of cars starting to form at the toll booth.

Chrissy studied his profile. "Can I ask you a question?"

Quinlan glanced at Chrissy and raised his eyebrows, "If it's not too hard."

The rain pelted the window and made it very hard to see. "You didn't much care for my grandfather, did you?"

"Is that a question?" Quinlan looked in the rearview mirror to see if he could pass the lane of cars that were backed up in front.

Chrissy leaned toward him, "Are you avoiding the answer?"

"No, I didn't much care for him."

"What about my grandmother?"

Quinlan turned the wheel into the right lane, which was free now. "Your grandmother was a very nice lady. Frankly, I thought she deserved better."

"So you think that ..."

"That's enough for today, Detective Rosen. I need to concentrate on that." He pointed up ahead to a four-car pile up that reduced traffic to a slow crawl while police motioned for oncoming traffic to get into the right lane.

"No more questions," Chrissy said as she looked out the window through the rain-soaked windshield.

The rain pounded the window next to Buddy's bed.

His visitor straightened the sheet under his neck as he

lay sleeping. His head turned slightly and he grimaced when he tried to move slightly to the right. He lay back down with his chin upturned and his shoulders slumped. The visitor leaned across his bed to look him straight in the face.

The door opened and Tyrone looked in.

The visitor jumped slightly as did Tyrone, who said, "Well, I'll be. I didn't even see you come in, ma'am."

"I hope you're not mad at me," Andi said as she looked up at Tyrone. Knowing what the answer was to be. "I didn't see anyone outside of the room, so I thought I'd better just come in and see Buddy."

"Well, ma'am, I was going to say the same ... I hope you're not mad at me for leaving the post. You know Officer Sambito hasn't come back in a long time. I don't quite know what to do."

"Did he say where he was going?"

"He said something about a cup of coffee. But that was over an hour ago."

Andi looked down at Buddy and then back at Tyrone. "You know, since I'm here, why don't I just watch over him while you look for Mr. Sambito? I don't mind."

"That's nice of you, ma'am, but I really think that I should be ..."

"Nonsense, besides you need to find out just what happened. Call for reinforcements while you are downstairs." Andi got up and gently pushed Tyrone through the door. She saw another hospital security officer coming toward them. "Look, here comes an officer now. He can stand outside while I stay in here with Buddy." Andi closed the door on Tyrone.

"What was that all about?" Lanie North asked as he walked up to Tyrone.

"Strong-willed young lady, that's what that is. Stay here a second, Lanie, while I go downstairs to look for the cop Sambito. Don't let anyone in unless they're on the list." Tyrone handed Lanie the clipboard.

Lanie took it reluctantly. "Ty, I'm on break. I was just coming to tell you ..."

"And I am very glad you told me that. Now stand right here for 10 minutes." Tyrone walked quickly to the elevators before Lanie could complain.

Andi sat down again very gently so as not to wake Buddy. She had her large purse on her lap. That was the bag that she loved so much. It carried tons of art supplies. The "catchall" bag, she called it. The kids used to dig through it during class, with her permission of course, and find items she would purposely leave for them. There might be a piece of clay wrapped in cellophane just ready for those exploring hands to give it shape; or maybe there was a set of old keys that had unique designs, so great for ink imprints or relief impressions. Some days there were candy bars, dozens of them, for everyone.

Today, there was a gift for Buddy. She carefully placed a .44 Magnum on her lap and slipped her bag back down on the floor next to her. She looked down at Buddy sleeping and a tear crossed her cheek.

"I do love you, Buddy." Andi said it so quietly that she could hardly hear it herself. "I wanted to tell you the truth so many times. I couldn't then and I can't even now. It hurt me so when everyone deserted me. I felt that you were my only friend after they took away my dad. Why didn't you try to find me? I thought you loved me. I was out of my mind. It took me years to recover ... hospital after hospital. You know, Buddy, it's funny."

Andi started to walk around the room holding the gun and gesturing with it to make her points. "You are the one who has the nightmares now. The horror you felt at seeing your best friend run down by a car ... feeling guilty about not being able to help ... his screams haunting you every night ... your tears and your sweat ... all these years ... you feel so sad." Andi shook her head and looked out the window.

"I don't dream, Buddy. Do you know that?" Andi turned to Buddy and now talked above a whisper. "I don't dream at all. I sleep like a baby. Can you believe that? The pain is still there, but not when I sleep. Your friend, Max. I remember Max. He was close to you. I wanted to be Max. I wanted to be there right next to you. I wanted to comfort you when your dad hit you. I wanted you to ... to ... love ... me."

Andi broke down sobbing and collapsed in a heap on the windowsill. The gun was at her side. Her other hand covered her eyes.

The door opened and Andi turned quickly to see Ramon Martinez enter the room. She slipped the gun into her coat pocket. "Sorry," he said. "Didn't mean to frighten you." He squinted in the darkened room. "Is this Buddy Rosen's room?"

"Yes ... yes it is."

"Wait ... you must be Andi, right?"

Andi nodded her head.

"You are every bit as beautiful as he said you were." Ramon walked over to Andi and shook her hand. "I am Ray Martinez. I've known Buddy forever."

"You are with ... Save the Beaches Foundation ... right?"

"That's right."

Ramon walked over to Buddy's side. "Buddy, my friend, you've had a rough life. Can't get a break, can you?"

Andi started to wake him up. "He's been pretty out of it."

"No, no ... let him sleep. I just wanted to see him." He walked closer to Andi. "Are you familiar with our Foundation?"

"Buddy mentioned some things about it. You raise money to protect the beaches right?"

Ramon laughed quietly. "Yes, that we do. We are also known as SOBs" He shows Andi the SOB ring on his finger. "Buddy never wore his ring. His dad did, you know? The ring stands for Sons of the Beaches. That's us: Sons of the Beaches. No women — sorry, nothing personal."

Andi was getting slightly nervous at Ramon's sudden haughty tone. She wanted Sambito to come back to check on them.

"Buddy's father and my father joined with a powerful senator to keep us safe. Protect our beaches. It takes money and power to make things happen, you know? We had a strong workforce of men that came from across the United States — visitors to our beaches, who became the founders: the original SOBs. They pledged support and put the SOB Foundation as a beneficiary in their estate plans and insurance policies. They knew that when they passed on, the work would still carry forward."

"Sounds very ... honorable."

Ramon dropped his head. "It was ... it was."

"That's bullshit!" Buddy opened his eyes and looked directly at Ramon. "It was anything but honorable, Ramon. Abe left me documents that showed how your honorable founders ran the Foundation. How they decided when it was time to get more money and who should die to give them cash. It was full of graft and corruption. Abe's motel was at the center and the Foundation was a convenient pass through that was protected."

"Really, Buddy?" Ramon paced the room. "And I suppose you have evidence that shows graft and corruption?"

"Abe documented it all. Frances wrote about it in her diaries."

"All the SOB members that died were all from natural causes or accidents," Ramon said as he grabbed Andi from behind and put her in a choke hold. He took out a knife and placed it next to her throat. "All the deaths — except for yours, Buddy."

Buddy tried to sit up but felt the searing pain in his chest.

"Ray, you bastard! Your dad was a good man. But you ... you turned down the path of greed and ... shit ... and The Motel ... is mine ... you know it ... Abe left it for me in his will."

"Oh really? You must have seen an old version. The documented will is with our attorneys. Phillips made sure it was ironclad. The Martinez family controls both the Foundation and the motel. Wait a minute. The Martinez family, that's me, isn't it? And poor Phillips. It was his time ... I liked him. But he is not with us anymore. Had a bad accident I heard ... in a subway station."

He kissed Andi on the cheek. "Andi here is really Audrey. But I'm sure you have figured that out by now. Audrey went psycho a few years back after losing her father and running away from her foster home. Arrested for vagrancy and theft and a few other things." He whispered to Andi: "Did we try a little prostitution perhaps?" Andi tried to pull away but Ramon increased his grip.

"So … let's see: Psycho bitch hooks up with the son of Abe Rosen, who she detested and blamed for the death of her father.

"She is spurned and ashamed. She leaves this note …" He reached in his pocket and put a note on the table. "… and slits his throat as he lies in bed. She then slits her wrists and dies slowly while her boyfriend bleeds to death."

"I don't like that ending," Andi whispered through the pressure on her neck.

"Really?" Ramon laughed and loosened his grip while he moved toward Buddy.

"Really," Andi said as she pulled out the .44, cocked the trigger and shot Ramon through the temple.

The door slammed open violently. One vested officer in SWAT team gear fell to one knee and pointed his rifle at Andi's heart. Another officer slipped inside the room and held a revolver pointed at her head. Quinlan followed in slowly with his gun drawn.

Andi looked up. The gun was still at her side. Buddy was stretched across the bed looking at Andi and back again at Quinlan.

"Drop it, Audrey!" Quinlan's steely blue eyes seared right through Audrey Jennings, daughter of Ralph, the slow-witted handyman; lover of Buddy Rosen, who was in the middle of another nightmare as he lay there awake. Audrey Jennings felt herself turn back inward to that mute child who felt so much pain.

Buddy quietly said. "Audrey ... saved my life."

CONFLICT:

Quinlan Shows His True Colors In the End

Chrissy's head felt like it was in a vice. She woke up to the sound of city workers fixing the road outside the house. Looking up at the alarm clock, Chrissy noticed it was close to noon. Rolling over to the other side of the bed, she slowly dragged herself to the bathroom.

"I think I've aged 10 years overnight," Chrissy said as she looked at herself in the bathroom mirror. Brushing her teeth was a bigger challenge. She couldn't feel her gums. Her contacts were killing her. She left them in overnight and her eyes were practically swollen shut. She popped them out and put them in their cases.

Chrissy slipped on a pair of socks, boxers and an undershirt. She padded out to the kitchen, peeked in on Buddy, who was resting comfortably, still rehabbing from the hospital.

Where had the time gone? It had been two weeks since the Ramon incident. Putting together the pieces of the puzzle finally gave her father some peace, but opened new wounds. Ramon Martinez was his biggest disappointment. It was Ramon who tried to kill Buddy. He knew that Buddy had more than enough evidence to put them all away and take his precious hotel. He shot him with his own gun. Buddy had long since forgotten that Ramon borrowed it months earlier for Margarita's protection.

Chrissy had worried about all that her dad had to deal with — especially Andi.

She had held his hand when they escorted her to a treatment facility. "Daddy, I'm so sorry ..."

Buddy put his fingers on her lips, "Chrissy, there's a small cardboard box under my bed. Would you get it for me?"

Chrissy walked to the bedroom and bent down beneath the bed. She had to almost lie prone to reach the small box. Chrissy placed it in front of Buddy as she kissed him on his cheek.

"What was that for?" Buddy asked with a sly grin.

"I had to wipe my mouth on something." She playfully slapped his shoulder.

Buddy lifted the lid of the box and pulled out a headless doll and a diamond ring. He handed them to Chrissy.

"Audrey's?"

"Audrey's."

"Then you knew. You knew she was really Audrey."

"I've known from the beginning. I found these under my bed after she moved in."

"And you never told her."

"I didn't have to. I understood her pain and I knew that she loved me." Buddy lifted a picture from the very bottom of the box. The black and white had turned to sepia tones, but you could still see the image. Buddy stood in his baseball uniform with his bat at his side, and Audrey stood next to him clutching her doll and looking up at his face, smiling broadly.

She was glad he was home now and smiled as he slept.

Chrissy put on a pot of coffee and took a bagel out of the package. She needed her glasses, desperately. She could hardly make out the writing on the bagel package.

"Okay," Chrissy said as she rummaged through her knapsack pulling out items, "where are you guys? Here's my chapstick, my brush, a two-week-old cracker, Certs, and — wait a minute — what's this? "The package from Abe dropped from her purse. Chrissy looked at it she tore it open. There were documents: insurance policies, financial statements, a scribbled envelope for her dad — and a single film canister.

"Well, I'll be. I forgot all about you."

She tiptoed into the bedroom and placed the letter on his dresser next to his pillow. Then she fished out her glasses and headed toward the living room. The movie projector was still set up from the week before, which now seemed like light years ago. Chrissy threaded the film through the sprockets and clicked it on...

... the image flickered and the frame was soon filled with blue.. The camera pulled back and three fisherman were standing in a small boat waving and drinking beer. Bennett was one and Philips was another. The third had a hood on. The camera swung around and caught another fisherman with his back to the cameraman, focused on fishing ...

... suddenly the frame filled with snow and another shot blurred into focus. Wobbly camera angles showing the legs

of one of the fishermen. Then there was a shot of the floor of the boat ...

... The hooded man came into the shot and images of him choking the solo fisherman came in and out intermittently. The camera was apparently shooting a scene that the cameraman had not planned ... it appeared that the camera was thought to be turned off and he was holding it while the action was taking place. Suddenly there was a splash as the fisherman was thrown overboard by the hooded man who now had his hood down and his face was clearly seen ...

The feeling of fear and nausea gripped Chrissy's stomach. The face of the murderer was so clear. There was no mistake.

It was Quinlan.

"Coffee's ready," Quinlan was standing right behind Chrissy, holding a cup of coffee in one hand and keys in the other. "Chrissy, how many times have I told you not to leave the keys in the front door?" He smiled.

Chrissy jumped.

"Chrissy, Chrissy ... you really should try it. It gives you energy in the morning." Quinlan circled around the living room table as Chrissy circled the other way. The projector kept running as the film slapped around the reel. He reached the projector and undid the movie reel. He put it in his coat pocket and turned toward Chrissy with his gun pointed at her.

Chrissy swung one of the dining room chairs and hit Quinlan as soon as he turned. It knocked the gun into the air and sent Quinlan spinning into the wall. Chrissy ran to the front door and clawed at the locks. Quinlan came behind her and pushed her head into the door. Chrissy slid down the door, holding onto the knob for dear life. Quinlan had her neck in his hands and dragged her to the kitchen, pulling her hair at the same time.

He threw her into one of the kitchen chairs. "Now," he was breathing heavily, "as I was saying, maybe coffee in the morning would get rid of that irritable feeling you get sometimes."

She looked at him with one eye starting to shut, "Who was the man ... the man you — killed?"

"Nobody you would know: just another SOB. His time was up. Too bad that I have to kill you too, Chrissy. I really didn't want to."

"Who else did you kill? Did you kill those sisters? "

Quinlan stopped her. "One sister. Remember, one was already dead."

"Did you do it for the jewelry?" Chrissy asked as she watched his hand on the gun. All she could think about was something she had seen in the movies. If you keep them talking, they won't shoot. She only hoped he went to the same movies.

"No. That was just smoke and mirrors. I left enough clues to get poor Ralph. It was much more complicated." He grabbed her hair. "That's enough talk, Chrissy."

He raised the gun to her heart.

"Wait...at least tell me the story. You owe me that."

Quinlan thought for a minute, then peered outside through the blinds. "I owe you nothing. I've killed people, Chrissy. I'm not proud of it. I wasn't born to do this. I don't even know how I let myself get to this point, but that's just the way it happened. One more death won't matter."

Chrissy squeezed her eyes shut. "I didn't ever really like you Detective ... but ... I never took you for a murderer."

He paused again and dropped her into a chair. "Aw shit ... I had two kids, a wife, a mortgage, a crappy police salary. I was offered an opportunity. I thought I would finally get some standing in the department. I thought that this would be my chance. Even more impressive was that I would directly report to Senator Bennett, one of the most powerful men in the Senate. I remember my captain calling me to his office. He sat me down and said, 'Mike, I've got a special assignment for you. No one else can know about it, not even your family. It's a high-level security position. You are to meet these two gentleman today at one o'clock for details. Interested?' "

Quinlan reached for his cell phone as it buzzed. He turned off the ringer. "Where was I? Oh yeah. So I met with Bennett and his little faggot aide who told me that special assignments are vital and need to be handled with the utmost security. I was one of the chosen few. They also said that these assignments aren't always 'legal,' but they protect all their operatives and I needn't worry. But I did ... worry. I asked a lot of questions but didn't really get straight answers until I "signed up." By then, of course, it was too late."

"Was Mrs. Katz an assignment?"

"She was a casualty. You might say, curiosity killed the Katz," Quinlan laughed cynically, "The Senator and his mistress used to spend some time at your grandfather's motel, where he shared some intimate and not so intimate secrets. The Katzes happened to be in the wrong place at the wrong time."

"Why did you kill my grandmother?" She searched his face for reaction. Quinlan stopped.

"I didn't kill Frances. Abe did." Quinlan looked at the ceiling. "I loved her. She was going to go away with me. Abe couldn't handle it so he strangled her."

"How did you know?" Chrissy saw a chance. If she could keep him talking long enough she might be able to distract him and run to the door again. This time she would get a head start.

"I was there. She gave me a note the night before to tell me that she was going to tell him at the boat dock. I wanted to be there. I was just … too late."

"So you drowned him?" She adjusted her chair so that she was a little closer to the door.

"I hit Abe with a rock when I heard her scream. Since they were both dead, I thought I'd make it look like a boating accident." Quinlan stood up to stretch.

"Too bad the bastard didn't really die then. Showing up here when he did caused the real trouble. When your dad got those films and the evidence started to mount up, I had to …"

Chrissy lunged for the door. Quinlan reacted and put his shoulders into her ribs, knocking her into the refrigerator. He stood over her as she wept on the floor.

"Anyway, as I was saying before I was so rudely interrupted, I had to clean up the mess. I'm sorry you had to be the final chapter."

He pulled back the hammer and a deafening explosion rang out. Chrissy looked up as Quinlan fell forward over her legs. The shot had discharged on the floor right next to her.

Leaning on the door frame, Buddy stood with a baseball bat at his side.

Chrissy kicked Quinlan's lifeless body over and grabbed her dad. She cried on his shoulder as he helped her to a chair.

She barely noticed the sting in her left half-closed eye as the tears ran down her cheek.

Buddy was crying too. He held the scribbled note in his hands and started to sob uncontrollably.

"What was it, Dad? What did Grampa Abe say in his letter to you?"

Buddy's voice faltered. "He wrote the scores of every baseball game I ever played."

The End

www.ingramcontent.com/pod-product-compliance
Lightning Source LLC
Chambersburg PA
CBHW060603310726
48982CB00008B/1218/J
9780578514642